HIGH STAKES

Carolyn Hart

Oconee Spirit Press, Waverly, TN www.oconeespirit.com

Library of Congress Cataloging-in-Publication Data

 Hart, Carolyn. High Stakes / Carolyn G. Hart. ISBN 978-0-9859107-8-5

This is a work of fiction. All of the characters, organizations, and events portrayed in this novel are either products of the author's imagination or are used fictitiously.

    1. Romantic suspense fiction. 2. Historical fiction.

The text paper is SFI certified. The Sustainable Forestry Initiative® program promotes sustainable forest management.

Cover design by Kaitlyn Tucker. Cover image © Randy Hines.

This book is dedicated to
Lesa Holstine, a mystery authority

1

"THE SENATOR LOVES BLONDES. All kinds of blondes. Majestic, petite, athletic, artistic." The speaker spoke authoritatively, enjoying this moment of power. "He especially likes classy blondes. You know the kind – tall, leggy, Nordic."

The paunchy man behind the desk nodded slowly. He had an air of somnolence, of immobility, but his cold slate-gray eyes reflected a quick intelligence. His gaze moved from the papers on his desk to the speaker, quick as a ferret streaking across refuse-littered ground. "So he likes blondes." His voice was surprisingly high for a man of his bulk He had a tight, pursed mouth that slowly stretched into a semblance of a smile. "Let's find him a blonde. Quickly."

Kirsten studied her glossy composite— a full-face picture on one side, a series of role shots on the other. The pictures were very good, but they should be. She'd certainly paid enough for them. They hadn't been good enough, because she was running out of money and the composite hadn't brought any callbacks.

She looked at the full-face side critically – ash blonde hair, Mediterranean blue eyes, chiseled aristocratic features.

Abruptly she grinned – a gamin grin that added life and warmth and a striking effervescence to her face.

"Dime a dozen, lady," she said out loud.

She knew her appraisal was true, both for the pictures and for here in Los Angeles. The streets teemed with beautiful women and she was just one more. It wasn't arrogance or conceit to recognize her own attractiveness. It was more on the order of a top tennis player realistically assessing her backhand. Beauty was the basic out here, but by itself it wasn't enough. Kirsten felt confident she had what it took to be a star, but she wondered if she would ever have the opportunity to prove it. She never expected to be a *big* star like Sally Field or Gilda Radner, but perhaps, just perhaps she'd find her spot in the sun.

Sighing, she slipped the glossy composite back into the folder. She had to make a decision quickly. Her bank account was teetering on the edge of extinction and not even beautiful blondes can write hot checks in L.A. and get away with it, not that she had any desire at all to write hot checks. That would be the last thing she'd ever do.

She put the folder down on the car seat and picked up The Hollywood Reporter. She got out of the car, locked the door behind her, and turned toward the beach, hurrying past the swimsuit and surfboard shops, already catching the wonderful, fresh smell of the ocean.

She'd always liked that song, the old one about all the best things in life being free. Sometimes, it was true – feeling the riffle of the sea breeze against her face, breathing deeply of the fishy, salt-laden air, feeling happy and young and eager. She was a good actress. All she needed was a chance to show her stuff. She knew it deep inside with a rocklike certainty.

But lots of things weren't free and if she didn't find an acting job pronto it was back to waiting— or worse, home to Minnesota, a failure.

She waited for the light to change, then crossed 101 to the sidewalk leading out to Huntington Beach pier. Sand gritted beneath her sandals as she turned down the broad steps leading to the beach. She stopped at the first concession stand and bought an order of strips and a Coke. Balancing the cardboard container and the drink, she bent down and slipped off her sandals and tucked them beneath her arm with the tabloid. She picked her way across the soft, hot sand among the bronzed bodies scattered like a tumble of manikins. The beach was packed. An August day at Huntington Beach brought out family groups, teenagers, senior citizens, and a long curving line of surfers who looked like black dots against the horizon. Most of them wore wetsuits because the water was very cold despite the August sun. The sand began to burn her feet, so she finished the crossing in a series of hops until she reached the narrow strip of damp sand, hard packed by the tide.

Kirsten sat down cross-legged, not worrying about the sand on her white cotton pants. Usually, she munched on the chips and stared out across the water, knowing that it was a highway to wonder, stretching from Huntington Beach to Singapore, but today she didn't have time to relax. She flipped open the tabloid and folded it back to the classifieds and began to read. Her eyes skimmed down the column, then stopped.

She read the ad twice:

WANTED: BLONDE ACTRESS, CHALLENGING ROLE, EXCELLENT PAY. Call 307-8025.

Excellent pay. Kirsten looked at the ad doubtfully. Nobody ever offered actresses excellent pay. But that was what the ad said and she certainly needed a job.

Kirsten finished the chips and licked sauce from her fingers.

Excellent pay.

Kirsten made a couple of wrong turns and looked anxiously at her gas tank gauge. It was just a blip above empty and she had four dollars in her purse. If she didn't get the job…. She shook her head determinedly. That wasn't the way to think. You had to have confidence to prevail. She was going to walk into that casting agency like she owned the world – or at least a good part of it.

The casting agency was in an older building on Doheny near Sunset. She liked this part of Los Angeles. It still had an aura of the 1930's, when glamour and California were synonymous and everyone knew that Sunset Boulevard was magic. The Chinese Theater wasn't far away. As she parked, Kirsten wondered what it would be like to step barefoot into soft cement. That fantasy entertained her all the way up the street. Once inside the building, she knew she was in the right place. A long line of blondes wound down the hall and up the stairs to the second floor. Kirsten took her place at the end of the line and hoped she wasn't too late. Once up the stairs and inside the casting agency door, she handed over her composite to a harried-looking woman in a shapeless Mexican dress, who handed her a questionnaire. Kirsten fished a pen out of her purse and scrawled St. Paul, Minn., in one blank and her birthdate, May 3, 1958, in another. She shot a curious glance at the blondes near her and wondered how many fudged that question. Sometimes she didn't like being in a business that equated success with youth, but she was young now and she would worry about tomorrow when it happened. She reached the line that requested educational background. She always hesitated to fill it out because she was afraid Vassar sounded too New Yorkish and fancy for Hollywood, but she'd learned honesty a long time ago from a man she admired very much so she carefully printed the answer. Would it help to say she'd gone on a full scholarship? She shook her head a little. She was sure whoever read this couldn't care less. She put down history as her major, then wrote industriously on the several lines provided for job experience. She did have something to brag about. She'd had bit parts in three soaps and she'd had real hopes that something further might come of her appearance on *Jet Set*, but so far the character was scheduled for only two episodes. She really liked that character, an intense, striving young lawyer torn between love and ambition.

"So what's the deal? Do you know?"

The nasal twang cut through Kirsten's thoughts. She looked up at the blonde (not natural) in front of her.

Kirsten shrugged. "All I know is what I saw in the paper."

Her new friend shifted gum from one cheek to the other. "So every blonde in L.A. pumped over here."

"It looks like it," Kirsten agreed.

The girl offered her a stick of gum and Kirsten declined.

"Gee, sometimes I think I'll go home to Amarillo. All I got out here is calluses from standing in line and a proposition from every guy who's seen the inside of a studio."

Kirsten grinned. "The starlet's lament."

"Well, it's no joke," Amarillo said grimly. "I'll bet you've had your share."

"I blow them off," Kirstin said lightly.

The line jolted forward and Amarillo turned away.

Kirsten finished the questionnaire, but she was thinking about what Amarillo said. Actually, no one had tried to proposition her in a long time and she knew why. She sent out a very definite signal nothing doing here, and that had been true ever since Aubrey. Suddenly some of the sparkle went out of the morning. Would she ever again be able to love? Would she ever again be able to trust any man enough to share her heart? Aubrey had hurt her and she was still wounded inside. She felt very remote and aloof and extremely unwilling to gamble with her heart. The stakes were too high.

"Next."

She looked up with a start, realizing it was her turn to be interviewed. She knew what counted at interviews so she lifted her head, smiled, and walked confidently through the door.

The heavy-set man behind the shabby oak desk watched her enter and gestured for her to close the door. His face was expressionless, stolid, and, somehow, forbidding. He held out a pudgy hand for her questionnaire. Her composite lay on the desk in front of him.

As he scanned the questionnaire, Kirsten looked around the small room that held only the desk and one straight chair as furnishings. Behind the desk and a little to the right, a door to an inner room was ajar but no sound or movement came from it. Perhaps it was a storage area. A mirror hung on the wall to her left, but Kirsten knew she looked fine in a scoop neck white blouse, swirling peasant shirt, and new white sandals.

"So you went to Vassar."

His voice was surprisingly high for a man of his bulk. Kirsten tried to decide whether his tone was hostile. It was hard to tell. Actually, he sounded faintly bored.

She nodded.

"You majored in history." It was a statement, not a question. Then he asked briskly, "What period?"

The question surprised her, but she answered pleasantly. "Classical. Emphasis on first century Rome."

His eyes dropped back to the questionnaire, then lifted to appraise her.

Kirsten felt a wave of revulsion as his cold gray eyes seemed to devour her, studying her face then dropping, slowly, the length of her body, but she realized it wasn't a lascivious look. It was a measuring, testing, evaluation look.

"Okay," he said abruptly "Do your stuff."

Kirsten didn't need a script. When she could pick her own monologue at an audition, she always did a speech from Scene II in "The Taming of the Shrew". And when she did, it always took her back for an instant to Vassar and to Avery Hall and the musty old theater and her freshman year. She knew Kate's part, knew the rolling, vigorous lines from heart.

She paused for a moment, closing her eyes, bringing Kate to life, feeling Kate's anger and heartbreak and passion. She could feel Kate pulsing within her. Kirsten stepped back a pace, turned to face an imaginary Petruchio, and began to speak.

"Nay then, do what thou canst, I will not go today! No, nor tomorrow! Not 'til I please myself. The door … "

When she finished, she stared haughtily at her imagined foe, her face uplifted and scornful.

The man behind the desk sat there stolidly his heavy face expressionless. Then he glanced down at the questionnaire and made a check mark.

Kirsten's shoulders sagged a little. She'd done it well, as well as she'd ever done it in her life, and he sat there like a lump of dough. Her car was almost out of gas, the rent was due and, if she didn't get this job …

"Call back in two hours." The words were uninflected, showing neither interest nor approbation, but, obviously, she still had a chance.

When she returned in two hours, there was only one other woman in the waiting area. They looked at each other warily and didn't speak.

The other woman was called first and Kirsten wondered if that was a good omen or bad?

Then it was her turn.

This time the heavy-set man behind the desk watched intently as she crossed the room. When she stood in front of him, he asked, "Kirsten Soderstrom?"

She nodded.

"We'll need you for a couple of weeks and you'd better understand — this is a tough role, it's physically demanding and you have to play it 24 hours a day.

Kirsten stared at him. She wasn't new to auditioning, and this wasn't following the pattern. She couldn't count the times she'd auditioned, sometimes at casting agencies, sometimes at theaters on bare stages that seemed immense in an empty auditorium. There would be a director or an assistant in charge of casting, and sometimes even a producer. This time there was only this heavy-set, expressionless man in an office oddly bare of furniture – and people. The back of her neck prickled.

"What's going on?" she asked quietly.

For the first time, his face changed expression. His small, tight mouth spread in a humorless smile that was perhaps even more unpleasant than his usual stolid demeanor.

"Quick, aren't you?" he replied. He was still smiling when he reached into his back pocket and pulled out a wallet and flipped it open for her to see. "Ellis Kemp, FBI."

Kirsten looked at the open wallet and the FBI shield. All she felt at first was a surge of exasperation. For heaven's sake, she was caught up unwittingly in some kind of investigation and she'd spent gas money she didn't have and wasted time in her search for a job She shook her head "I don't know what you're looking for, but I'm an actress who has to find work and …"

"Then maybe you'll take our job."

She frowned. "What could I possibly do for you?"

"We need an actress, a bright and smart girl who can follow orders."

"To do what?"

"Play a role just like you would on the stage. You'll get a closet-full of clothes, a car, and a thousand dollars a week."

She managed not to say wow, but she felt it. A thousand dollars a week would certainly solve her cash flow problems and it would give her another shot at the brass ring. She wouldn't have to stand on her feet eight hours a day in some coffee shop and she wouldn't have to go home to Minnesota.

She studied him for a moment, but she didn't like him any better than she had the first moment she stepped in that office. "Why me?" she asked sharply, She gestured toward the now-empty waiting room "There were a hundred blondes out there. Why are you picking me?"

He shook out a cigarette from a battered package of Lucky Strikes. "You're exactly what we're looking for, a classy blonde – tall, slim, beautiful. You're the kind of woman our man likes."

"Our man?"

Kemp took a deep drag on his cigarette "Look, whatever we tell you from this point on is confidential. You can tell us yes or no when I've explained it, but you have to give me your word that you won't ever reveal to anyone what you're going to hear now."

"Why would I tell anyone?"

"Some people like to be big deals. They like to get their names in the paper and hope the publicity gives them a boost."

"I'm not looking for that kind of publicity. I'm an actress. All I really want is a good job."

"So, you'll keep quiet?"

"Of course."

"Okay, it's simple enough. You know what a sting is?"

She nodded slowly, "Some public official has his hand out and you're going to set him up,"

It was very still in the bare room. The heavy man cocked his head to one side. "Now, how did you know that, little lady?"

Little lady. The appellation went out with hoola hoops – and women as second class citizens – and she wondered what its use told her about FBI Agent Kemp? But he was the man with the job.

Did she want this kind of job? She thought about it as she replied. "My dad was a prosecuting attorney."

He glanced down at the questionnaire, "In St. Paul?"

Kirsten nodded.

The cold gray eyes moved to her face. "How do you feel about your dad's job?"

It took Kirsten a long moment to answer, not because the answer was hard, but because the tense was wrong. Her loss was still recent enough to bring an ache to her chest and the hot sting of tears to her eyes. She could picture her dad so clearly in his smoky, linoleum-floored office, a big Scandinavian man with powerful shoulders and vivid blue eyes and a tough face. She knew the truth behind that craggy face, the enormous compassion and the absolute bulldog-strong determination to see justice done. Always.

Kirsten swallowed. "My dad died last year. In July. A heart attack." She paused then continued quickly, "I admired him more than any man I've ever known."

The tension seeped out of Kemp. "So you won't have any qualms about catching a crook?"

"None." But she might very well have qualms about how they were going to catch a crook, using her. She intended to be very clear on this point. "Exactly what do you want me to do?"

"It's simple. You're a beautiful woman. This man enjoys beautiful women, especially blondes. Your job is to attract him and get his trust. Then, at the appropriate time, you will make a search of his study, looking for cash. Lots of it."

"Just what am I expected to do to attract him?" she asked carefully.

The tight little mouth curved again in a small smile. "Relax. You can play it any way you want to. He's a gentleman." There was a sardonic inflection on the last word. "He won't expect you to fall in bed with him. Look, you're an actress. Play it like the beginning of a love story. All you have to do is get friendly enough with him that you can get into the house and manage a little time alone in his study. We realize it may take a while, but we're prepared to pay you a thousand dollars a week while you have a good time. And you'll have a good time. He's full of charm."

Kirsten felt a curl of distaste. She'd known a lot of charming men and that didn't say a lot for them. Aubrey was very charming. But she wasn't going to be paid a thousand dollars a week to like this man, she was going to be paid a thousand dollars a week to act. It would be a tough role, but she'd never turned anything down because it was hard to do. Besides, she didn't like crooks.

There was one final question.

"Who's the man?"

2

"SENATOR JACOB HOLLAND JOHNSON."

Kirsten knew her face revealed both shock and dismay, but it was the last name she would have expected to hear.

"Do you know him?" Kemp's heavy face was intent, still.

Slowly, Kirsten shook her head. "No, not really. I saw him once at a rally in Long Beach."

She remembered that afternoon so clearly. It was several years ago when he ran his first campaign. She wasn't even particularly interested in politics. It was chance that brought her to the park that day. It was crowded with senior citizens, some playing croquet, others sitting on park benches, most listening to the band that played in the band shell. Then the music stopped and a well-built, dark-haired man moved through the crowd, smiling, shaking hands, stopping often to bend down and listen to questions and comments. She hadn't stayed to hear the speech because the race meant nothing to her. She was new to the state then and not yet registered to vote, but she carried away a picture from that sunny afternoon of a vital and commanding man with a ready smile and intense dark eyes, a man who seemed truly to care about the old people who reached out to touch him.

"I thought … He seemed attractive." She was surprised at the sharpness of the disappointment she felt. After all, she didn't know him. He meant nothing to her so why should she care that he was a sham?

She cared because she'd liked him on that sunny afternoon. She'd felt a quick and certain empathy with him and ever since she'd followed his career and been pleased at his successes and wished him well, all because of that one glimpse on a long-ago afternoon.

"Who's he taking money from?" Her voice sounded harsh and angry.

"Armatec, Inc."

"Who's that?"

"A defense subcontractor. Armatec manufactures the parts for a certain bomber — if the Senator's subcommittee chooses that bomber."

Kirsten understood very well indeed what Kemp meant. As head of a sub-committee Johnson would wield tremendous power over what would or would not be included in a final defense bill.

"Armatec's in trouble," the heavy man continued. "If they don't get to make the parts, they'll go bankrupt. If they do – it will bring in about $300 million."

"But he's rich, isn't he?"

"Johnson?"

She nodded.

The agent smiled. "Is anyone ever rich enough?" Then he shook his head. "It's hidden money, don't you see? He doesn't need it personally. Hell, no. The Johnsons own half of the San Joaquin valley, but this is money he can dole out during an election. He can buy precinct workers, that kind of thing."

It was funny, she thought, what people would sell their souls for. For some, it was money, pure and simple, but for Jake Johnson it must be a hunger for power.

"Are you willing?" he asked finally, after a long silence.

Her father had spent his life fighting crooks. This wouldn't be a pleasant task for so many reasons. She didn't like deception of any sort, and she especially didn't like the idea of dishonesty in any kind of personal relationship. But she didn't like crooks and she felt a commitment to justice that her father would have understood and applauded.

"I'll do it."

That's when he gave her the folder.

The heavy-set man behind the desk waited until the door closed behind Kirsten, then he called out. "She's gone."

He didn't turn to look as the door behind him opened, but his slate-gray eyes watched as the new arrival sat down in the straight chair in front on the desk. "What do you think?"

"Perfect. Jake will go to his slaughter like a lamb."

There was a particularly nasty tone of satisfaction in the description, Kemp thought. He looked at his conspirator with his face still expressionless, but he felt a wave of disgust. There was so much enjoyment in that smooth voice. "She'll go to the slaughter, too."

The only answer was a shrug.

Kemp began to lift himself out of his chair. "Let's get out of here." Once, a long time ago, he would have felt sorry for the girl, but he no longer felt sorry for anyone. It wasn't part of his life.

Kirsten liked to carry a script down to the beach. She didn't mind sand or running children or even the skimming hazard of out-of-control Frisbees, so she carried the folder and sunglasses and a thick, soft terry cloth towel along with her low-slung beach chair and set up not far from the pier pilings where there was a little less traffic.

She was determined to treat the blue-backed folder just as she would a script, but, when she opened it, she felt again that sharp ache of disappointment.

He was so extraordinarily attractive. He wasn't conventionally handsome, not as Aubrey was. Jake Johnson was distinctive, his lean face as memorable as a sharp-visaged Roman profile. She could imagine him crouched in a chariot, the reins taut in his hands, a slight smile on his full, sensual lips as the horses thundered around the dusty arena. Perhaps it was his mouth that revealed him, that indicated the flaw in character that made him seek a secret hoard of cash. His lips were full, strong – the mouth of a man who enjoyed every pleasure.

A series of photographs filled the first several pages of the folder. The first was a formal picture, one she recognized from campaign posters. He was smiling and the smile seemed to be reflected in his dark eyes. His face was sharply planed with high cheekbones and a blunt chin. His face had interesting angles, a kind of unexpected angularity that was arresting and impressive. He looked as though he could be very charming – and a very tough customer in a struggle.

She flipped through the rest of the pictures, several in a sailboat with the rugged coastline of the Monterey Peninsula in the background. His brilliantly black hair was tousled by the wind and his teeth flashed against a tanned face. He wore racing trunks in these pictures and she remembered that he had been a champion butterfly swimmer on the Berkeley swim team when he was in college. He was 37 years old and just as lean and well-built as when he was a college swimmer, his chest broad, his legs powerfully muscled. Another picture showed him astride a horse. He wore a rolled-brim Stetson and he might have been a cowpuncher riding into Laredo, looking for whatever the town could offer. There was that aura about him, of controlled strength, of a restless, seeking hunger.

Impatiently, she flipped through the rest of the photographs. She knew, for heaven's sake, what he looked like, and she didn't need to dwell on his attractiveness, because he lacked that basic most important quality, character.

Her eyes dropped to the text. She skimmed the paragraphs. He was born in Santa Rosa. He was elected to Phi Beta Kappa at Berkeley, received a master's in economics from Stanford, and a doctorate from Harvard. He'd taught at Stanford, then begun his political career with a race for the Assembly. From there, as they said, it was history, a whirlwind campaign for the Senate and election as the youngest man ever sent to the Senate from California.

Her reading slowed. The heading was bland enough, PERSONAL INFORMATION, but the information itself was beyond even the meatiest in popular magazines. It indicated exhaustive surveillance and access to someone who knew him very well indeed.

It described his marriage that ended in divorce three years earlier.

Publicly, the Senator is always good humored when his former wife, Francesca Montez, is mentioned. Actually, he is very bitter about the failure of the marriage and attributes it to her ambitions as an actress. He never goes out with actresses and is privately scornful of people who, as he puts it, "earn a living by playing charades." He takes good care, of course, not to express this view publicly since, obviously, many of his most powerful constituents earn their livings in just that fashion.

Kirsten laid the blue-backed folder down in her lap and looked up to stare out across the water. It was a cloudy day and the water looked sullen.

So he didn't like actresses. That, of course, was why the agent had quizzed her so extensively on her college background and why they'd worked together to create a career for Kirsten. She'd taken a lot of notes toward the end of that meeting. She knew who she was supposed to be and that would be part of the challenge. Could she carry it off? The agent stressed that the Senator liked intellectuals, women with quick minds, well educated, able to discuss the world of both today and yesterday. She'd been a history major at Vassar, with especial emphasis on ancient history, and, most particularly, Rome.

Actually, she'd always thought it would be fun to write a book about famous Roman women and their effect upon their times. At perhaps no other period in history had women wielded as much power and been afforded as much independence as during the days of Imperial Rome. Americans of the 1980's would, in many respects, have felt quite at home in first century A.D. Rome – and there were a good many corrupt Senators then, too.

Her eyes dropped again to the folder.

He liked jazz, Brubeck and Monk, and his favorite food was Mexican, Santa Fe style. He still swam two miles every day, in the ocean when in California, in the Senate pool when in Washington, D.C.

But the information which perhaps surprised her the most was the description of him as a very private, almost reclusive man, intensely devoted to his career, working ten-hour days, seven days week. He rarely socialized. When he did, he often dated Eloise Bishop, an old friend from college days who ran a public relations agency in Washington.

So how was she going to meet this man who didn't like actresses and, except for his appearances as a Senator, shunned the public eye?

Kirsten looked out at the heavy gray water. There was a heaviness of the air like the sense of oppression and doom, and it reflected her uncomfortable feeling of voyeurism, of poking into private places.

But Jake Johnson was a crook. He was betraying people who trusted him, who sent him to the Senate to represent their interests. He'd forfeited his right to be secure from intrusion in his private life.

She flipped back to the photographs. There were three of Francesca Montez. Kirsten knew, of course, what she looked like. She'd seen her last film, *Carnival*, which had been talked about as a possible Academy Award winner. It hadn't made it, but Francesca Montez's career was flaming. Kirsten looked down at one particular picture, Francesca's face half-turned toward the camera. She had raven dark hair, as dark as the Senator's. They must have made a striking couple, and Kirsten was surprised at her feeling. It couldn't be jealousy, for heaven's sake. What did it matter to her that Jake Johnson had apparently loved passionately this exotically lovely woman? Not at all, of course. If he now liked blondes only, dated blondes only, that indicated how very much Francesca had meant to him. And, after all, Kirsten wasn't required to have the Senator fall in love with her. She had only to attract him enough that she could gain access to his study and search for the money.

The narrow scope of her assignment and the breadth of information collected about the Senator made it very clear that they knew him to be guilty. They must have chapter and verse of who paid him and why to be confident the undercover operation would require only the search of his study.

Kirsten bit her lip. Why should she feel sad to be convinced that the case against him must be irrefutable? He meant nothing to her. That long-ago glimpse of him at the rally in Long Beach was a fragment out of time and, obviously, the attraction she'd felt for him was just part and parcel of the manufactured charisma cultivated by politicians, especially corrupt politicians.

Abruptly, she slapped the folder shut and stood and dropped it into her chair and rolled up her towel and put it down for a weight, then turned and walked swiftly across the sand. She didn't care that the breakers were foaming higher than usual. The surf was up but she felt a sudden desperate need for strong physical exercise. She began to run, buffeting herself through the waves, pausing and diving beneath the big waves until she was just past the first wave. She swam parallel to the beach, feeling the greedy tug of the outflowing tide, but she was a strong swimmer. The briskly-cold water made her stroke faster, harder.

When she struggled back toward the beach, she felt invigorated, extraordinarily alive. She liked a challenge, the tougher the better. As she toweled off and slipped into her terry cloth robe, she looked down at the blue-backed folder. It was in there, everything she needed to know. She gave a decisive nod and picked up the folder. The agent had said she'd receive a call in a few days.

The wind rattled in the palm tree outside her bedroom window. Kirsten moved restlessly in her sleep. She was walking down a broad staircase. A chandelier glittered in the hall beneath her. A man stood at the foot of the stairs, waiting, his face upturned. He was smiling, but it was the formal smile of a campaign poster. He was a poster not a real man. Then the poster moved, took shape, and Jake Johnson stood there waiting, and she began to hurry, plunging down the steps that grew steeper and steeper. Suddenly he turned away, and she saw him reaching out and an incredibly lovely, darkly sinuous woman moved into his arms, held him in a tight embrace. Kirsten stopped on the stairs and she called out, "He's mine, he's mine!" She ran faster. She would catch them. She would. Her long white dress billowed out. Her heels tangled in the dress and she stumbled and realized she was falling headlong down the immensely steep stairs, falling, falling, falling …

She woke with her heart thudding, terror hammering at her mind. She struggled to break her fall, then realized it was a dream. She lay stiffly, gasping for breath. It was a long time before the feeling of horror seeped away. It was the weather, of course, just the weather. When the rain came, the oppressiveness would lift and she wouldn't feel so threatened, but sleep was a long time coming. As she lay there, Jake Johnson's image moved in her mind, but this time he wasn't smiling and his dark eyes were cold and hard.

Kirsten balanced the grocery sack on her hip while she fished in her pocket for the door key. She whistled soundlessly. The storm had finally broken and the morning had the fresh, clean scent of the ocean, the way California should smell, not the way it so often did when the hills cupped the smog in a low-hanging sulphurous haze. Kirsten had used some of the money advanced to her by the agent to pay the rent and she'd splurged that morning at the open-air market, buying Mahi-Mahi fresh from Hawaii and, best of all, an abalone steak.

She would put her groceries up then fix a sandwich, a split sandwich, a split croissant filled with dill cream cheese and parsley and go to the beach on this wonderful, gorgeous day and master the rest of the material in the blue-backed folder. Last night's bad dream was only a vaguely discomforting memory. Everything was super fine this lovely …

She stopped midway through the door and stared at the manila folder lying in the center of the small room. She looked back at the door, at the key still in the lock.

The door had been locked. She was sure of that.

She looked carefully around the small living room, poised to turn and run, but it lay quiet and empty, the sun sparkling through the east windows on the rattan couch and the two red canvas-backed director's chairs. From where she stood, she could see the tiny kitchen with its white wooden table and two straight chairs and the old-fashioned white enamel refrigerator and the two-burner gas stove. She turned her head a little to the right and the half-open door that led into her bedroom. Carefully, she put the sack down on the floor and walked softly across the room and pushed the bedroom door open all the way. The closet was too small to hide anyone and the bedroom was empty.

Slowly, she started to breathe again. The apartment was empty save for her. Whirling around, she reached down and picked up the manila envelope. Again, she looked at the front door.

The envelope had been placed in the center of the living room and that meant human hands placed it there.

Someone had been in her apartment.

She'd known it, of course, the instant she saw the envelope.

It was a larger-than-average manila envelope, at least 10 by 14 rather than the more common 8 by 11. However, it felt light, almost as if it were empty.

Kirsten pulled out the flap. She opened it and found a single sheet of white paper. She read the message, but it did nothing to assuage her anger. They had no right to come into her apartment. They could have left a message in her mailbox. They could have called. Instead, without a by-your-leave, someone had unlocked her door, walked in, and left the envelope. Was that all they'd done? She felt at the mercy of forces she couldn't control.

But, after all, they were on the same side and perhaps this was only a matter of caution, a determination not to leave information where anyone else conceivably could see it.

They should have asked. The thought was stubborn and still angry.

The message did, however, answer the question she'd wondered about for several days. Now she knew when her adventure would begin.

3

KIRSTEN POURED A GLASS of orange juice then she split a bagel and spread it with cream cheese. The single sheet of white paper from the manila envelope lay on the white wooden table. She pulled her freeway map a little closer to be certain of her route. Why had they set up a rendezvous so far from where she lived? But they were paying for her time, that was for sure, so a two-hour drive on the freeways was just part of the bargain. She'd gotten up a little earlier so she'd have plenty of time. She knew how traffic could back up. She'd take Beach up to the San Diego Freeway then turn north on San Gabriel .…

The ring of the telephone startled her. Who in the world could be calling? More than likely it would be someone wanting to sell venetian blinds or solar heating. She didn't exactly rake in the personal calls. She'd concentrated on Aubrey to the exclusion of anyone else. For her friends, it was a sad reality in L.A. that when you were working you had oodles of friends, and when you weren't the phone never rang.

She lifted the receiver.

Mia's voice rippled over the line like water cascading down a mountain stream, full of sparkle and life.

"Kirsten, I called you first. Listen, it's a great chance, a chance to work for Denver Hedrick— and you know what that can mean. I mean, I know he's got this reputation, but I'm sure he can't be that bad, and, who knows, maybe it would be fun, or, if not fun, sometimes you have to …"

Kirsten was laughing as she answered. She could picture Mia, her flyaway red hair practically standing on end, her cat green eyes glistening with excitement and sheer pleasure in living and being Mia.

"Whoa, slow down. Chance to do what? And what does Denver Hedrick have to do with it?" Who he was, of course, was one of the hottest directors in town, with a magic touch at finding people with money who wanted to spend it in Hollywood.

"A chance to try out for his new film – and it has two female leads. Young female leads. Why not us?"

Kirsten was truly touched. Not many hungry young actresses would dream of sharing news of that kind with a friend who might end up competing for a role. She'd met Mia last spring when they'd both worked on several episodes of *Jet Set*, and they'd immediately become fast friends. It was like that. When you worked in a show, the other cast members were your family and you spent your free time with them, and everyone was bound up in what they were doing. When the play ended or your role in an episode, then you just as immediately drifted apart, remembering each other at first, then forgetting as new friends took their places. Right now, Kirsten was between shows and between friends – and it meant a lot to her that Mia had called.

"Oh, I wish I could," she said quickly. "I really do, but I've promised to meet my aunt in Carmel. She's coming out on vacation and I really can't get out of it. I may even be gone a month, but I'll call you, Mia, as soon as I get back in town."

"Gee, I didn't even know you had an aunt. Oh Kirsten, I wish you could – this could be the break of a lifetime. Are you sure …"

Kirsten felt a pang, but she'd already paid the rent with some of the advance money. She didn't have a choice.

After Mia rang off, Kirsten stared at the phone for a long moment. She almost reached out to call her back, but she didn't have enough money in the bank to repay the advance. Besides, they were counting on her. Resolutely, she reached for the manila envelope and slipped out the single sheet and began to read, once again, the terse instructions.

Okay, she could do it.

First, her costume.

She studied the slacks and shorts in her closet. She was meticulous about her clothes. She considered them part and parcel of her attack on the world – an actress always had to look right, whatever the circumstances. This morning, she was to be the all-American tourist. In California, the all-American tourist wore shorts or informal pants and tee-shirts and sneakers or sandals. Kirsten pulled down light blue walking shorts and a multi-striped tee-shirt. Light blue Keds completed the outfit. She dropped her sunglasses in her purse, then slipped the blue-backed folder into the manila envelope as her instructions had ordered. She paused at the front door. Had she forgotten anything? Oh yes. She picked up the freeway map from the coffee table and dropped it into her purse, too. She drove to Beach and turned into the first convenience store and bought the latest copy of *Time* magazine, again as she had been instructed. She slipped the manila envelope into the center of the magazine, and she was on her way.

It was a good two-hour drive. Trips like this always reminded her just how enormous greater Los Angeles was; but, finally, and she was in good time, she turned off the Ventura Freeway onto Rosemead, then onto Huntington. She glimpsed old and lovely homes, most of them Mission style, set back on immaculate green lawns bordered by enormous eucalyptus trees. She'd visited the Huntington Art Gallery and Museum before. The Library contained the famous Ellesmere manuscript of Chaucer's *The Canterbury Tales* and two of the surviving twelve copies of Shakespeare's Sonnets. It contained much more, of course, but these had captured her imagination. She'd visited with a group and no one else cared very much, while Kirsten could have spent the day. After she completed her assignment this morning, she'd go to the Library. But for now, her goal was the Art Gallery. As always the long walk to the Gallery was a delight in itself. To believe people had once actually lived like this. Kirsten knew that Southern California was a world of mansions, but the Gallery, which originally was the residence of Henry E. Huntington, was in a class by itself. This was when people lived in the very grand manner. The house reflected the fabled days of its construction, the nineteen-tens when America was still young enough to feel that there was no limit, would never be a limit, to national wealth and accomplishment. The pillared main entrance glistened in the soft morning light, and graceful urns decorated the second-floor balcony. The red-tiled roof and white stucco walls seemed to shout. This is California.

Kirsten bought her ticket and entered the Main Hall. She glanced at the porcelain vases and eighteenth-century English furniture but didn't linger, turning right to go through the Dining Room and the North Passage to the Main Gallery. She walked midway down the long room, then paused and looked at *Blue Boy*. She'd been there before, yet the painting always had the same effect, the effect of any magnificent work of art, a sense of wonder at human accomplishment, at the gift of eye and hand that had created a masterpiece.

Only a few other early-bird tourists roamed in the long, quiet gallery. Kirsten saw the bench positioned in the center of the room opposite *Blue Boy*. A woman sat there. Kirsten walked slowly toward the bench. A new copy of *Time* lay beside the woman.

So, this was it.

Kirsten strolled toward the bench. She kept her gaze on the painting, but she was very aware of the woman, who had iron-gray hair drawn back tightly in a bun which emphasized her pointed face. She wore a bulky gray coat-sweater, several sizes too large, and shiny sunglasses and seemed to be staring impassively at the painting. She wasn't, Kirsten thought, a particularly attractive person. Slowly, Kirsten backed toward the bench and sat down, never taking her eyes from the painting, but she felt electrically aware of her seat companion. Casually, Kirsten placed her copy of *Time* atop the other. Then she stood and walked closer to the painting as if studying the brush-marks. In a moment, when she turned, the bench was empty except for one copy of *Time*.

Kirsten took care of all the details that afternoon, telling her landlord she would be away, picking up her laundry from the cleaners, returning some library books. Making the arrangement to be gone reminded her how alone she was. She had no family to notify. The aunt she described to Mia was imaginary. Her mother had died when she was a child, and her father last year. Her college friends were scattered from London to Honolulu and her actor friends were will of the wisps. She hadn't talked to anyone from the last show except for Mia. When she got back from this job she'd redouble her efforts to get a role, and, more than that, she'd join an aerobics class or go to a great books discussion at the library. But, for now, the future was set.

After she was packed, and again she chose her wardrobe carefully because now it was very important that she dress for the role, she heated a Lean Cuisine and flipped on the TV, ready to study her instructions one more time. The public channel flickered on.

Kirsten sat very still in her chair, and wondered about luck and fate and chance. Senator Jake Johnson seemed to be smiling directly at her. He wore a soft charcoal suit and, of course, the regulation TV blue shirt. His blue rep tie was perfect and his smile was singularly attractive. It seemed to promise a combination of confidence and wry self-deprecation. He leaned forward and gestured with a short, hard chop of his hand.

"I'll fight that. I'll stake my career on it."

The camera switched to a smooth-faced commentator with a warm smile and cold eyes. "Now, Senator Johnson, will you really oppose legislation proposed by your close friend, Senator McKeen?"

Johnson grinned and the white flash of his teeth against his tanned face brought forth an image of health and good humor and vigor. "I sure will," he said bluntly. Then his smile faded and he looked serious and even a little sad. "No one could value friendship more than I. I admire Senator McKeen. We've often worked together in the past. But I will oppose this bill with every ounce of my strength. We owe the public absolute candor about our personal finances ..."

Kirsten leaned forward, listening intently.

" ... and I am going on record about that. Serving in the United States Senate is a sacred trust. We are public servants, and we must be willing to undergo the strictest scrutiny."

The commentator smiled. "Another time, Senator, I'd like to pursue this topic with you and with Senator McKeen if possible, but our time is up tonight and I would like to thank you for your willingness to appear on the Randolph Report. And now ..."

Kirsten snapped off the set. As the image faded away, she looked down at the sheet of instructions. Everything she needed to know was there. It was time for the play to begin. She knew her role, but she didn't have that opening night sense of delight and excitement and panic because she remembered a flashing smile and eyes filled with laughter – and integrity.

Of course, she thought cynically, he would act honest. All crooks do that. But nothing could diminish the power of his personality, the deep richness of his voice, the humor in his dark eyes.

She took a deep breath. Now was no time for second thoughts. She had a role to play. It started tomorrow.

4

KIRSTEN PULLED THE TILLER. The wind puffed out the brightly striped sail and the little boat surged ahead. She frowned a little in concentration because the wind was tricky, the way it blew around the headland. If she didn't maneuver just right, she was going to end up on the rocks. She leaned forward, her hand firm on the tiller as she judged the strength of the gusts, and played out enough sail to sweep her out beyond the headland. With the rocks safely behind, she spanked across the ridging waves and scanned the horizon, oblivious to the crisp beauty of the day. She didn't exactly have butterflies. It wasn't an opening night sort of feeling. It was more a sense of caution, a feeling that she must exercise the care and precision of a glasscutter. If she made one wrong move the pattern would be ruined so, very definitely, it was up to her not to make any wrong moves.

The sailboat reached open water and she saw the yacht, glistening in the August sunlight like a Cartier diamond. Apparently the Senator liked all the good things in life.

Then she saw him.

He was a larger man than she'd thought from that one long-ago glimpse and from the photos and his appearance on television. He stood at the stern and it was unmistakably him. That sharply angled face, the brilliantly black hair, ruffled now in the breeze, the broad chest and shoulders and powerfully muscled legs. He was gazing off into the distance and she wondered what he saw. Fabled cities or mountains to climb? The loveliness of the darkly-wooded peninsula or the thundering surf of Carmel Bay? He had the air of a man in control, sure and certain of his destiny, and well he might, because he was a United States Senator and his actions and efforts affected each and every American. Kirsten took a deep breath. That was why she was here, and now was the moment for the play to begin.

Kirsten yanked the tiller, then a sharp gust of wind tore it from her hand and the small boat wavered and capsized. As it heeled over and she was flung out into the icy water, she screamed. She struggled up through the cold water, then floundered at the surface as a poor swimmer would and saw him react and had a moment's appreciation for his immediate response. He might be a crook, but he certainly didn't hesitate if there were a life to be saved. He was climbing up onto the railing and his swift, easy grace reminded her that he had been an athlete, was obviously still an athlete. He dived smoothly, a sharp, shallow racing dive, then he was stroking powerfully through the water, his arms moving in unison in that most spectacular of all strokes, the butterfly, and he was at her side and a strong arm slipped around her body and she was being pulled effortlessly through the water toward the yacht. She felt the firmness of his chest behind her and wished suddenly, unaccountably, that she had really had an accident, that this was not a clever charade on her part. When they reached the yacht, he grabbed the dangling rope ladder and pulled her around to face him. Sputtering, she looked up into his face.

That darkly memorable face glowered at her. "Why the hell don't you have on a lifejacket?"

He didn't give her time to answer. Instead, Kirsten found herself being hauled up the ladder like a CPR dummy.

He plumped her to her feet and she stood on the gleaming deck, water streaming down her face and dripping from her drenched shorts and soggy blouse, and she realized he was glaring at her with the same enthusiasm he might display for a sack of eels.

She looked up into his angry face. He certainly was much bigger than she'd thought and he was obviously very fit and strong. She remembered, so clearly, the strength of the arm that had held her and wished that he still held her. He looked incredibly powerful and magnificently male as he frowned, black hair glistening from the water, stocky shoulders hunched forward. He looked as though he'd like to toss her right back overboard.

"No lifejacket," he said angrily. "Do you know how deep that water is?"

She had to answer. She had to play her role, attract this man, earn his trust, but she couldn't find a word to say. She felt flooded with sensations, many of them quite different from anything she'd ever felt before. She had, in her life, been attracted to men but never in quite this way, never with quite this sense of excitement and fascination and intense awareness. There were more handsome men. Certainly Aubrey, with his sleepy green eyes and actor's mobile face, would be accounted a handsomer man, but she had never felt this stirring of delight and desire with Aubrey. What was the fascination of this man who frowned down at her, looking as though he'd like to wring her neck? Surely it was nothing more than the carefully cultivated charisma of a man who was accustomed to seeking and wielding power. Yet, in her heart, in her immediate, visceral response to Jacob Johnson, she knew that wasn't the answer so she stared up at him and, for once in her life, had absolutely nothing to say. She'd rehearsed this moment in her mind, planning the kind of lithe, seductive movement she'd employ, the femme fatale aura she would project, yet now she stood helplessly on the polished deck, her pink cotton blouse plastered to her, her soft white cotton shorts clinging, her blonde hair streaming down so that she looked like a freshly beached mermaid, wanting desperately to say something to erase his scowl.

Deep inside, in her innermost being, in that private place where only the truth will do, she knew that she wanted him to like her, wanted it desperately, and she knew, too, that her desire had nothing to do with the reason she stood on the deck of his yacht.

All the fine, clever words had fled her mind. The lines she'd rehearsed seemed tawdry. This man wouldn't like that kind of approach. There was something about him that precluded the shallow and meretricious. What fool, what insensitive, blind fool had written that report on him, including all kinds of deeply personal material, yet, apparently, not ever understanding his true nature? That report reflected the writer's baseness, not Jake Johnson's.

Still he frowned, his dark eyes glistening with anger. Kirsten stared up at him. Would she ever see him smile? How would a smile soften those full lips? His uneven, rugged face was taut with anger but she thought she'd never seen eyes that held more life and intelligence and humor. She liked everything about him, the way the sunlight glistened on the dark hair on his chest, his aggressive stance, the feeling of leashed and volatile strength. Her liking, her deep and instinctive response, transformed her face, changing its grave reserve to warmth, and she began to smile.

Abruptly, she stuck out her hand and said, "Okay, I know. I'm a damned fool and I'm sorry and you should have let me sink to the bottom. But I'm glad you didn't." She looked at him appealingly. "Can we be friends?"

Jake Johnson's friends and enemies both agreed on one thing in their appraisal of him – he could make up his mind in an instant and respond with lightning reflexes. For once in his life, his manner would have confounded both his friends and enemies. He stood on the deck, his legs apart, his head bulled forward, a dark frown on his face. It had seemed so clear just a moment ago. Some damn fool woman was out in a tricky spot where she had no business to be and managed to dump her sailboat, then she turned out not to be wearing a life jacket, thereby proving her incompetence. Vitriolic words whirled in his mind and he was ready to let them rip. His opponents in the Senate knew the power of his tongue and he never hesitated to make his position, on any issue, perfectly clear.

But now she stood staring up at him contritely, and it was like having Aphrodite drop in for tea. It was magical, as magical as an Irish mist on an autumn morning or the faintly-heard strains of a violin on a darkened street in Rome. She was stunningly, breathtakingly lovely, ash blonde hair that glittered like wet silver, a fine bone structure that emphasized the haunting beauty of deep violet eyes, eyes so deeply blue they brought to mind the vivid glitter of Horace's emerald dark sea. Her face would have been severe with too much the aloof grandeur of a goddess except for the soft fullness of her mouth. He wanted to touch her mouth, feel its silken pressure against his.

She was smiling at him.

What would she do if he reached out and pulled her close and kissed her? The thought and what it implied about his feelings shocked him so much that he felt his frown increase.

The smile began to slip away from her face and she looked uncertain, as a child might if a door slammed in her face.

Abruptly, and he did it without thinking, he reached out and took her hand and felt an explosion of desire within him and wondered desperately where his usual control had gone. Instead of shaking the hand she had lightly offered, he held it tightly.

Kirsten shivered.

His eyes dropped to her clothing and he knew she was cold as the dancing breeze cut through the wet cloth. It took a long moment for him to speak because he was looking at the soft roundness of her breasts so clearly outlined against the pink cotton and the delicately feminine curve of her hip and thigh, and the pulse of desire again shocked him with its intensity.

"You're cold," he said gruffly, and knew he sounded hostile. "Look," and he tried to soften his voice. "I've got some dry shorts and shirts and things down in the cabins. And even a clothes dryer in the galley. No sense in your freezing."

He forced his eyes back to her face. God, he had to get himself under control. She wasn't a goddess. She was a damn fool with wet stringy hair who was beginning to shake with cold – and her hair shone like moonlight on a mountain lake and her body was as perfect as any woman ever carved by Michelangelo, but she wasn't marble, she was a living, breathing woman – and he was still holding her hand. He let go of her hand abruptly and turned and moved toward the companionway, and heard her follow.

He stopped at the door to the main cabin and held it open for her. She brushed by him to enter and, once again, he was agonizingly aware of her nearness and the smoothness of her skin and the way her body curved. He rummaged in the top drawer of a chest and pulled out a pair of nylon gym shorts and a tee shirt and handed them to her, then he backed out of the cabin and shut the door.

He carefully measured out coffee, his favorite Columbian, and put it in a percolator. As soon as she came out and he could dry her clothes, he'd take her back to the marina and this unsettling episode would be over and done with.

Inside the cabin, Kirsten slowly pulled off her sodden clothes and rolled them up and began to dry off with the thickly fluffy towel he'd found in a second drawer. She held the shorts and tee shirt in her hand for a moment, then shrugged. He didn't, of course, have panties and a bra to offer, but she didn't want to wear her wet underthings because she really was cold and still shivering. The warmth of the towel helped but nothing could help the confusion in her mind. The scenario wasn't going according to plan at all. There was no room in the script for her to be attracted to Jake Johnson, but human emotion couldn't be scripted. She knew that the FBI agent would be pleased because she clearly had Jake Johnson's attention, but it was a two-way street. She had never expected to have such an overwhelming emotional reaction to him. What was she going to do about it? Kirsten, she admonished herself, don't be an utter fool. The man is a pro. He plays people like drums. He probably turns on the sex appeal with every woman he meets and enjoys seeing them quiver like teenagers at a Michael Jackson concert. All right, she wasn't a teenager and she wasn't going to quiver. She finished drying off and slipped into the shorts, which were very brief, and the tee shirt. It was time to open the door and get to work and forget the wild fancies that had flooded her mind. Kirsten whirled around and opened the door.

He stood in the galley and, at the sound of the opening door, turned to look. Once again, they both stared at each other and Kirsten knew it was happening again and she mustn't let it.

She forced a smile to her face and walked toward him. "I'm terribly sorry to put you to such trouble, Senator."

The atmosphere in the cabin changed abruptly, became suddenly more formal. He smiled at her, but it was a practiced smile and she knew it was a public smile. He was disengaging from their rapport of a few moments ago. She knew that now was the moment for her to employ her wiles, the kind of sexual techniques of the second star, the villainess in a soap, but there was no way she could force herself to do it, not even if her mission failed before it began. Her mind was awash with contradictory feelings. He was a crook and she'd promised to help ensnare him, but every fiber of her being insisted that this man could do nothing shoddy or second-rate. She knew it instinctively, yet all the while her rational mind argued that appearances do deceive, that perhaps the most important lesson of adulthood is understanding the dictum that nothing is ever quite what it seems to be.

He poured coffee into two mugs and held one out to her. "You aren't causing me any trouble," As he said it, he knew he lied. She was causing him more emotional upheaval than any woman he'd ever seen, but he'd spent years perfecting absolute control of his emotions in public, smiling genially while inwardly outraged, nodding in formal support while suppressing amusement, attacking his opponents energetically for a constituent's pet proposal while personally disinterested in the outcome, and he certainly wasn't going to lose that control now. The new session of Congress would be one of the most important in his career. He needed to devote every ounce of energy and intelligence he possessed to mastering those new bills important to California, and most particularly the possible tax changes that could affect Silicon Valley and thereby California's best hope for future wealth— and this slim and lovely golden girl wasn't part of that future. Surely he'd learned with Francesca that there wasn't time for both career and love, not when you had a career as demanding as his. So he smiled again and knew it was his meet-the-voters' smile and was relieved. Now, to get this over with as soon as possible.

"You have the advantage of me, Miss ..."

"Kirsten Soderstrom."

"Miss Soderstrom. Are you on a holiday here in Carmel?"

Jake was pleased with the predictable, stiff conversation that followed, but it took all his willpower not to look down the long length of her legs, so fully revealed by the short, very short, nylon gym shorts, and to ignore the fullness of her unfettered breasts beneath the cotton tee-shirt. And when she reached over to hand him the empty coffee cup, he wanted for the first time in more years than he could remember to break free from his life, to be honest and open and vulnerable once again. But, my God, that was a young man's game and April only came once in every life. He took the cup and turned his back to her and waited until, once again, he was the public man, then faced her with a genial smile. "I imagine your things are dry by now."

Kirsten grinned. "Not only do you save my life, you do my laundry. Senator, I am truly in your debt."

"It's certainly been my pleasure." Pleasure. When the morning began, he would have laughed had anyone told him he would be acting like a moonstruck kid by mid-afternoon.

He didn't waste time, now that he was within minutes of freeing himself from this distracting and oh-too-attractive guest. He fished out the clothes from the dryer and gave them to her. When she came out of the cabin, once again fully dressed, he was waiting by the companionway, ready to lead the way upstairs. It didn't take long to maneuver the yacht close enough to the over-turned boat for him to right it and attach it to a tow line; then they were on their way back to the marina.

Kirsten stood a little to one side and watched as he steered the yacht. Now was the time for her to try to rekindle his interest. She knew what she should do and she even had an inkling of how to do it, but she couldn't bring herself to try, no matter whether she ever saw him again. She couldn't be false with this man and she knew what that meant, no matter how much trouble it caused her.

When the yacht rode at anchor beside the dock, he turned and looked at her. "I'd like to ask a favor."

How did she keep her face still, compose it in a look of polite inquiry? She managed it while thinking how she would love to please him in ways that would have shocked him were he able to read her mind. "Of course. Whatever I can do."

He looked a little embarrassed. "If you don't mind, I won't walk out on the dock with you. You see, I'm not supposed to be here."

"Oh," she said blankly.

"Actually, so far as my offices in Washington and San Francisco are concerned, I'm in New York this week."

She didn't let her face reflect her surprise, but she did ask slowly, "Do you mean no one knows you're in California?"

"Right." He grinned and looked suddenly years younger. "I do this sometimes just to keep my sanity. There's something wonderful about anonymity – especially after you lose it."

"How can you manage to keep it a secret?"

"By not telling anyone. That works every time."

"No one?"

A select few. A very select few."

Kirsten managed a light smile, but inside she felt cold. Her employers knew very well where he was, knew when he would be aboard a yacht off shore from Carmel. Who had told them? Someone among the select few? She didn't reflect her thought in her face or voice. Instead, she asked pleasantly, "So, you want me to keep your secret?"

"I'd appreciate it."

"Of course."

Then it was time to go. She knew it, but it was still hard to make the move, to say goodbye and leave him and know she would never see him again. Abruptly, she stuck out her hand.

They shook hands and she said quickly, "Thank you. For everything," and turned to leave. She took one step, two, three, and then he called out, "Kirsten, where are you staying?"

5

CONSUELO HUMMED A LITTLE tune. She enjoyed fixing meals for Jacob Johnson. Of all the Johnson children he was her favorite, though she would never have admitted it and she always treated him perhaps a little more sternly than the others. He knew, though. He saw past the prim fold of her mouth and her dignified demeanor to the love in her dark eyes and the pride. Now she watched the cocoa. It mustn't boil. Too much heat ruined cocoa. It must be just perfect, though she knew she made it for the boy of long ago and not the man who worked so late in the study on important matters. She felt a thrill of pride. Was there ever a young man grown to be so fine as her Jacob? A United States Senator. She frowned. He worked too hard and there was no play in his life. Even today when he'd gone out in the yacht, he'd taken a briefcase stuffed with papers. Still, he looked young and happy when he came in, younger and happier than she'd seen him in many years. She smiled and watched the cocoa and poured it at the precisely correct instant into a blue pottery pot. She put the pot and a mug and a plate with two fresh coconut cookies on the lacquer ware tray, then frowned in annoyance at the ring of the buzzer in the kitchen. She turned and hurried to answer the house telephone, and the swinging door closed behind her.

The door from the hallway opened slowly. The newcomer looked up and down the hallway, then stepped into the breakfast room and moved swiftly to the tray. It took only an instant to remove the pot lid and dump a tiny vial of liquid into the cocoa and stir. The hallway door was firmly closed when Consuelo returned, shaking her head in vexation at people who buzzed then left before she could answer. She picked up the tray and stepped out into the hall.

Kirsten walked up the street from her inn to a Hungarian restaurant and ordered cheese blintzes. She drank a glass of Chablis and thought what a waste it was to eat interesting food and drink wonderful California wine by herself. She knew the answer, of course. Since she'd met Jake Johnson, it would be a long time before she would spend time alone without thinking of how wonderful it would be to spend it with him, and that was an absurd way to feel on the basis of one afternoon.

The blintzes were probably delicious, but to her they tasted like straw because she kept thinking about the call she was going to make first thing in the morning. She couldn't spy on Jake Johnson. Would they put her in jail for accepting money under false pretenses? What if they insisted she pay for the accommodations here in Carmel? The blintzes suddenly felt like raw cookie dough in her stomach.

She turned down dessert and walked swiftly back to the inn, not even pausing to look in the tempting store windows. She'd already seen enough of Carmel to realize it was a shopper's paradise. There were old books, fine ceramics, paintings by famous and soon-to-be-famous artists, assorted fabrics, and what her dad would have called gewgaws, but very expensive gewgaws, such as painted wooden ducks, brass sculptures, shell wind chimes, and even gingham cats. If she could be in Carmel on pleasure, she would poke into the shops and savor the wonderful assortment of goods from every corner of America and the world.

But this was not a pleasure trip and every bit of excitement was gone, replaced by depression and dread. She was afraid to call and say she wasn't going to do the job she'd taken on. She wasn't quite certain what caused her to be afraid, whether it was the natural uneasiness about breaking a promise or whether it was deeper than that, something to do with the coldness in Ellis Kemp's eyes, but she knew what she was going to do.

When she reached the inn, she stopped at the desk to ask for messages. There were none, and the last little bit of hope died. She'd thought, that last moment when he asked where she was staying, that Jake Johnson might call. She smiled at the night clerk and hurried through the lobby and up the twisting steps to her room.

It was a lovely room, furnished in bright chintzes and oak furniture. She walked over to the balcony and looked out at the swimming pool, then turned and looked at the telephone.

Jake Johnson frowned at the figures on the yellow legal pad. There was a discrepancy there … He punched the sums into the calculator once again. It couldn't cost that much to replace one part. Or, if it did, there should be an investigation. His face was grim, intent. Once again the figures didn't jibe. He scrawled a blistering question on his legal pad. The Pentagon would have to do better than this if they wanted his committee to approve the supplemental appropriation.

He sighed then and leaned back in his chair. He'd worked all afternoon, ever since he'd gotten back from the marina. He hadn't even taken a break for dinner, eating from a tray at his desk, but he knew it wasn't just to get the work done. He'd wanted to be alone. He hadn't wanted to talk with anyone about his afternoon – and the hauntingly lovely girl with the full, soft lips and captivating smile. Why didn't he want to tell anyone about Kirsten? He'd avoided dinner with is mother and Drew and Amy just so he wouldn't have to describe Kirsten. Was it because he feared revealing himself?

There was no room in his life for a golden girl from the sea and if he'd told about his afternoon, lightly described his rescue, they would have exclaimed and asked about her and his mother would have said, "Why, Jacob, she sounds delightful. We must have her over for dinner." So he'd chosen the path of wisdom. No one need know about it. He would spend this working holiday and slip back to Washington and his life would be unchanged. Of course, that's what he would do.

He felt a wave of fatigue and looked down at the papers, then pushed them aside. That was enough for tonight. His hand brushed against the blue pottery pot, and slowly he began to smile. Dear Consuelo. Did she think he was still seven? Hot chocolate. He felt the pot. It must be fairly tepid by now. Abruptly, he poured out a cup. She did make the best chocolate he'd ever tasted – and he wouldn't for the world hurt her feelings. He drank down the cup, poured what was left in the pot into his cup, and finished it. He began to tidy up the desk, putting several notes into his outbox for Amy to type tomorrow, running over in his mind the conclusions he'd reached then, suddenly, he felt a warm sweep of sleepiness. He was tired. So tired. He left the desk and turned out the light and started upstairs to his room.

The tall wooden clock on the landing chimed the hour. One. Two. Three. A gloved hand twisted the knob and slowly pushed open the door. The darkly-dressed figure slipped inside, stood quietly for a moment to listen, then nodded in satisfaction at the sound of the heavy, slow breathing. The mouth twisted sardonically. Cocoa for the master. Hope he enjoyed it. A gloved hand rose and a tiny pinpoint of light pierced the darkness. For an instant, the light played on the sleeping man's form. Jake Johnson sprawled awkwardly across the bed in a deeply drugged sleep. The light lingered for a moment on his face, then danced over the rumpled covers to the bedside table and the clutter of contents from Johnson's pocket. The light focused on a key ring. The intruder walked confidently across the room and reached down and picked up the keys. They jangled a little in the still room, but Johnson didn't move. It took only a moment to make a wax impression, then the keys were replaced and the room was empty except for the sleeping man.

Kirsten jumped lightly aboard the sailboat. She smelled coffee from a nearby boat and envied the owners. They were on holiday, probably, and getting up to enjoy a good cup of coffee in the miracle of morning at Carmel-by-the-Sea. Were they lovers, looking ahead to their hours together? Or perhaps good friends sharing a passion for the sea? Then she grinned. The boat owner could be alone just as she was and possibly miserably unhappy this misty morning. Why did she have this tendency to imagine backgrounds and lives for people she didn't know? She wasn't sure, but perhaps it was the reason she loved to act, a means of sharing lives and understanding others. Perhaps, too, it accounted for her empathy with others which could sometimes be painful and frightening. It was that ability to sense emotion which helped her succeed as an actress, and it was that ability which was now puzzling her. The more she thought back to the day she was hired by Kemp, the more she worried about what he would do when she quit. And why should she feel this? What was it about that day that caused this sense of discomfort, almost of fear? As she eased the sailboat out of the marina, she recalled that day, that long and fateful day, and suddenly she realized that there had been a feeling of strain, an intensity right from the very first that was foreign to casting sessions and perhaps was that quality which first made her suspect the audition wasn't what it seemed.

Why should Kemp care that much about hiring someone to set up Senator Johnson? Why should he be so intensely interested in the outcome of their conversation? Kirsten shook her head impatiently. Wasn't she creating a problem in her mind as an excuse not to call Kemp? She had to call. She wasn't going to spy on Jake Johnson.

Then why was she procrastinating, and what was she doing in the sailboat just after dawn? This was crazy, nutty and pointless. He wouldn't be out on his yacht at this hour, and, even if he were, he didn't want to see her again. That was pretty clear, wasn't it?

The line of twisted cypresses on the headland looked misty and otherworldly in the early morning fog. Jake leaned against the railing and drank slowly from the mug of steaming coffee. His head ached liked hell. Funny, he'd slept so heavily, but he hadn't awakened refreshed. Instead, he felt tired with an odd kind of lassitude, but the air would make him feel better — and the coffee. He looked over at the briefcase on the table. He needed to study the Amraam specifications then return them to Washington by military courier. He frowned. There were some critical decisions to be made and it was his responsibility to inform the committee about the merits of this system. Usually, he couldn't wait to plunge into this kind of task, but this morning he continued to stand by the railing and look out across the water. There were still patches of fog and it was cold out on the water. There wouldn't be any reason for her to sail this early.

He took a deep, scalding swallow of coffee. For God's sake, what kind of fool was he, staring into the fog, waiting for a woman to appear, just like a schoolboy hanging around a classroom door? He didn't have time to waste and he certainly wasn't going to get involved with a beautiful young woman who didn't even have sense enough to wear a life jacket. But he pictured the softness of her mouth and the long, slim line of her legs and still he stood by the railing. He certainly wasn't going to get involved …

The fog shifted, thinned, and through the mist, a brightly-colored sail took shape, and the sailboat glided toward him. He leaned over the railing and shouted, "Kirsten, hey Kirsten!"

Sheer happiness flooded Kirsten as she climbed up the rope ladder. To find him seemed a miracle and made her fears of the night before seem foolish. He was smiling and, obviously, he did like her, she was certain of it. When they stood on the deck, he held her hand and she looked up into his dark eyes and suddenly found it hard to breathe.

Neither spoke. Instead, they stood so close looking into each other's eyes, and there was only the dull faraway boom of the surf and the sharp caws of feeding sea gulls.

"I didn't think I'd ever see you again," he said abruptly. "I was afraid you might have left Carmel."

"I hoped you'd be out on the water this morning," she said quietly, and knew that it revealed her.

"You came out because of me?"

Slowly, she nodded.

He smiled at that, smiled and gently touched her cheek with his free hand.

That touch, that light, brushing caress, ignited a sweep of desire within Kirsten. She stared up at his bold face, now so open and appealing, and wished that she could feel the pressure of his mouth and knew, as he looked down at her, that he felt the same hunger. She felt a touch of panic because she knew she was very close to reaching out for him – and the man was a stranger, really. She had to get control of herself. She was Kirsten Soderstrom, a very aloof and controlled woman, even in love, or what she had thought was love. Aubrey had pursued her for months and she'd liked him, then thought she'd loved him, but she had never felt this sweeping desire just because Aubrey stood near her. Love with him had been the result of practiced arousal, not an urgent, instinctive need, and, she felt suddenly certain, making love with Jake Johnson would be explosive and magnificent, akin to diving from a cliff or riding a kayak down turbulent rapids. And if she didn't say something, anything, soon, she was going to be in his arms.

"I don't want to interrupt anything," she said breathlessly, disengaging her hand and stepping back a pace and hoping that he couldn't read in her eyes what she felt about him.

"Not a thing," and he pushed away the thought of the bulging briefcase down in the saloon. "Look, have you had breakfast?"

She shook her head.

"I have coffee, cake doughnuts, even whole wheat bagels and lox."

She grinned at him. "Bagel and lox, of course."

As they went below deck, he asked, "Why, of course?"

"Because this is an adventure, and you can't eat something as mundane as donuts during an adventure."

He laughed at that and she loved the resonance of his laughter, deep and full of amusement. He had a nice laugh, without a hint of sarcasm.

When they sat at the galley table and spread cream cheese on the bagels and topped them with the pink, smoked salmon, Kirsten smiled at him in delight.

He poured coffee for them. "An adventure," he repeated. He tilted his head and studied her. "Do you look for adventure, Kirsten?"

"Not really. I never have before."

"But now?"

"Perhaps."

He frowned a little. "It's funny, but until you came out of the blue yester-day, I had my week planned, planned down to the last second, actually. Mostly work – and a break from people." He looked at her intently. "Can you under-stand that, the need to be private sometimes?"

"Yes." She felt as if she'd known him always, and she had a clear sense that he, too, was a very private person, a man who couldn't easily share his inner-most thoughts. "It's rather like acting, isn't it?" she said before she thought. "You have to spend so much time dong what is expected of a Senator, don't you?"

His quick frown reminded her abruptly that he didn't like anything about acting or actors.

Then his face smoothed. "You're right, of course. I perform. All Senators do – and I get damned tired of it. That's why I try to slip away when I can and come home without letting anyone know. It's a lifesaver, but not very adventurous or exciting – until you arrived." He looked down at what remained of his bagel. "But now I'm having an adventure, thanks to you. So, who are you, Kirsten Soderstrom, and where did you come from?"

6

THE QUESTION CAUGHT HER by surprise. She had her prepared answer, the one carefully created in her session with the FBI agent, but these weren't the circumstances she envisioned. He was looking at her with genuine interest and caring. He wanted to know about her, Kirsten Soderstrom, and she wanted him to know the truth and like – or not like – the real Kirsten.

But she couldn't tell him she was an actress, at least not until she had a chance to make him care and then, perhaps, if he cared enough, she could convince him that actresses, too, could fall in love – and love faithfully and well. Wasn't she, though, presuming a very great deal? Did he share her feelings of excitement and wonder?

Kirsten shook her head helplessly. "Do you always ask such difficult questions in the early morning?"

He looked intrigued. "Is it so difficult?"

She nodded. Finally, she said, and not lightly, "I'm a long way from Minnesota."

"Did you come to California seeking fame and fortune?" But he didn't ask it unkindly.

"Isn't that why everyone's here?" Again, she looked into his eyes, expecting boredom or even derision, but found understanding tinged with sadness. "I know," she said quickly, "you think we're all silly, the swarms of us who come wanting to be Steven Spielbergs or Sally Fields, but you must admit greatness happens and sometimes to very unlikely people."

"Carmel isn't Hollywood," he said gently. "Are you an actress or … "

She interrupted, and her answer was true but only partly true. She was going to reveal a dream no one else had ever known and she wasn't going to claim that she was writing a history of Roman women. She wasn't going to be phony with him. "I have an idea for a script. I've saved my money (and that certainly wasn't true) and I've come to Carmel to try and finish it. The story is set here."

He looked out across the bay. The fog was almost gone, only a thin gauzy film against the rugged cliffs. The dark, twisted cypresses and tumbled boulders and crashing surf created a scene of overpowering beauty combined with harshness and danger.

"What's the name of your script?"

"Murder-by-the-Sea."

He grinned at that. "Do you suppose the Chamber of Commerce would approve?"

"I haven't asked."

"Will you tell me about it?"

She told him the story then, and she'd never before shared it with anyone or shared her dream of writing scripts. It was hard to do. She stopped several times, and each time he prompted her to continue. When she finished, she waited for his comment and waited with a hard knot of anxiety in her chest.

Slowly, he nodded. "That's good," he said finally, "especially the part at the end when Maury's afraid it's her son."

"You like it? You really like it?"

"Yes. Do you?"

She understood his question. Dreams can be talked about, but following a dream to its end takes guts and commitment and a special kind of stubbornness. Did she have that? Did she believe in herself?

"I've come to Carmel to find out."

"I like that, Kirsten," he said firmly. "And I like you."

"Thank you, Senator."

He shook his head at that. "I'm Jake."

"Jake." She realized as she spoke that her voice was too soft, too husky, that it revealed with terrible clarity how he attracted her, but she couldn't bring the name back. She felt her face begin to flush.

Once again, there was between them a stillness that signaled pulsing, awareness. They looked into each other's eyes and Kirsten saw desire in his.

"I'd better go." She said it breathlessly and matched the words with action, slipping out from behind the table.

He stood, too.

She wanted him to reach out and stop her, but, at the same time, she was afraid. This was too much too soon. How could she have fallen under his spell so quickly? The dossier that she'd studied at Huntington Beach indicated he was very experienced with women, an accomplished lover, and a man who always gave the ladies a good time. That was what the dossier said and she'd better remember it, and remember why she was here. Whether she was willing to spy on him or not, the FBI was investigating him and she knew that such investigations were usually deserved. Wouldn't she be the world's biggest fool to ignore what she knew?

He reached out then and his hand brushed her arm, and it took every ounce of will for her to stand there as if nothing had happened when, in actuality, she was strung taut with awareness of him.

"I know you have things to do." She began to back away. "I'd better get back to town and get to work. Screenplays don't write themselves."

She heard the banal words, appalled, but she was almost to the companionway.

"Kirsten."

She paused.

He took a deep breath. "You're right. I suppose we both should get to work, but … I want to see you again."

She smiled. "I want to see you, too."

He wanted to see her because he liked her, the real Kirsten. She'd been herself with him, been honest and open – except for the fact she was an actress, and someday she would be able to tell him that and he would know she wasn't like Francesca Montez

"Then how about dinner?"

"I'd love that." She hesitated. "But if you don't want anyone to know you are here … "

"Good point. What I'd really like would be for you to come to the house."

At her look of surprise, he smiled. "I keep forgetting I haven't known you forever – and that you don't know everything about the Johnsons. I'm staying at my mother's house on the peninsula with several members of my staff. Mother's awfully good to put us up on short notice and she still loves to have me bring friends home." He grinned at that and she found it an endearing smile. "You'll come?"

"Yes, I'd love to."

Kirsten didn't work on her screenplay that afternoon though she'd had every intention of doing so, but first she wanted to talk to the FBI agent. She tried four times to call Ellis Kemp, using the number she'd been given in that first meeting, but every time the phone was answered by a recorded message asking her to leave her name and phone number. She wanted to tell Kemp she thought the investigation against Jacob Johnson was wrongheaded. When she thought about Kemp and recalled his cold eyes and general air of cynicism and weariness, she wondered whether it would do any good. He'd demand facts. Why wasn't the Senator involved?

Kirsten sat very still. That was the point, of course, to prove that Jake was innocent, and she was the person who could do it. All she had to do was complete the investigation, just as if she were working for the FBI. Then, when the facts didn't support the accusations against Jake, why, that would be the time to tell Kemp he was off on the wrong track.

But somebody was taking money. The FBI must be certain of that to plan a search of the Senator's study. Kirsten looked across the room. There was a tiny camera hidden in the side pocket of her suitcase. It didn't look like a camera. It looked like a silver compact, a thin and square one, but it was a cunningly disguised and very sophisticated camera.

She squeezed her eyes shut in concentration. Jake, the camera, the study, the dossier, Jake's unannounced arrival in California – sure, it was plain as could be. Her eyes opened in surprise. If Jake wasn't a crook, someone on his staff had to be – and Jake didn't know it. Kirsten felt a wash of panic. This was deep water, very deep water, and she was afraid she was in over her head.

The crystal chandeliers above the massive oak table glittered like clear ice in winter sunlight. The damask table cloth and pale bone-colored china and glistening crystal goblets provided an elegant background for the dinner. The food was delicious and everyone seemed open and charming and friendly, but Kirsten sensed an undercurrent of tension. Was it her imagination? Was it because she looked and listened so carefully to the conversation, seeking some substantiation, however slight, for her suspicions? But their dinner companions seemed to be exactly what they were, Jake's mother and his longtime staff members, devoted to him, friendly to her, and certainly not involved in a conspiracy to ruin him because that's what it would amount it.

Kirsten forced a smile to her face and turned to Amy Montgomery, Jake's personal secretary. "Is it hard to pull up and come across the country with scarcely any notice?"

Amy looked surprised at the question for just an instant, then her smooth, secretary's demeanor returned. "I've worked for Jake for almost thirteen years now so nothing surprises me." She looked unflappable with a soft cameo-smooth skin and wide-spaced, almond eyes that gave her a restful, soothing appearance. "New York one day, Chicago the next, San Francisco another. It's all in a day's work."

"A long day's work," Drew Wilkerson interjected with emphasis.

As the others laughed, Jake the loudest, Kirsten studied Drew Wilkerson. He sat across the beautifully-appointed table from her. He looked at ease in the magnificent room with its teak paneling and enormous marbled fireplace. He had a sleek and satisfied manner that reminded her of a banker, though she knew he was Jake's press secretary.

Kirsten turned back toward Amy. "Thirteen years," she exclaimed. Then she frowned. "But that's before Jake ran for the Senate, isn't it?

For an instant, there was a constraint at the table and Kirsten wondered if she had said the wrong thing. She also wondered with a hot, sharp pang just how far back Jake and Amy's relationship went and what it had entailed.

Jake's mother smoothly bridged the moment. "Kirsten, sometimes we feel like Jake has been in politics forever – and, actually, he really has. I want you to know that he ran for his first office at the age of nine – president of his home-room class in the third grade – and he insisted on campaign posters."

"Did he win?" Kirsten asked.

"Of course. Jake always wins." Mrs. Johnson smiled down the table at her son.

Kirsten liked Mrs. Johnson, although she sensed the older woman could be formidable on occasion. Her face was a delicate, feminine version of Jake's, a high-bridged nose and full, generous mouth and vivid dark eyes. She had his good humor, too, and shared with him an aura of invincibility. That, Kirsten felt, reflected their life. She'd told Jake she felt a long way from Minnesota in Carmel. She certainly felt a long way from Minnesota in the long, paneled dining room of the cliffside mansion that overlooked the Pacific.

Mrs. Johnson smiled kindly at Kirsten but her questions gently probed.

Kirsten found herself describing St. Paul and her family— the mother she scarcely remembered and her father.

"It takes courage to be a district attorney," Jake said admiringly.

"He was a very honorable man," Kirsten said quietly. "I admired him very much."

Once again, for a fleeting instant, she sensed an undercurrent of hostility or pent-up anger. She struggled to identify, to pinpoint the source of her unease. Then she wondered if her imagination, always vivid, were playing her false? Everyone appeared so normal and every day, so precisely what they were supposed to be. Mrs. Johnson was looking quizzically at Kirsten with just the right amount of interest for a newly-met guest. Amy Montgomery reached for her wine glass and Kirsten noticed that she wore rings on almost every finger of her left hand; and one of them, a blood red garnet, was in a memorable, antique gold setting. The number of rings faintly surprised Kirsten because Amy dressed so plainly. She wore a high-necked black dress with a ruffled lace collar that Kirsten judged to be at least last season's, if not the season before. Her eyes moved down the table to Drew then quickly away when she realized he was staring at her. What did she glimpse in his eyes in the instant that they looked straight at each other? Was it curiosity or something more than that? But of course he would be curious, he and Amy both. Their lives centered around Jake Johnson's life, and anything he did affected them. Of course, Drew would be curious about this unexpected dinner guest.

It was over dessert of fresh strawberries and cantaloupe with a wedge of Camembert that Mrs. Johnson worked the conversation around to colleges. And where had Kirsten gone?

Kirsten recalled her session with the FBI agent and his insistence that she present herself as the product of a well-to-do background because the Senator liked women from his own social level. She looked down the table at Jake and thought he was the most strikingly handsome man she'd ever seen. As her father often dryly remarked, "Handsome is as handsome does."

"I went to Vassar," Kirsten answered. Then she said, very clearly and distinctly, "On a scholarship. My father could never have afforded the tuition."

So now it was clear who she was and where she came from if there'd been any doubt in Jake Johnson's mind, but when she looked at him he was smiling and, slowly, she began to smile, too.

They went out onto the terrace for coffee and Kirsten knew she'd never seen anything quite so spectacular as the plunging cliff with its dramatic view of the sun-splashed Pacific. The setting sun was a fiery orange-red globe riding low in the western sky, gilding the basalt rocks and the foam of the crashing surf.

They drank coffee and talked desultorily, and all the while Kirsten felt taut and expectant.

Then Jake put down his cup and stood and looked at her. "I promised Kirsten I'd see her home early," but his eyes locked with hers and she knew what she saw in them.

His hand lightly held her elbow as they started down the steps to the path that would lead to the front drive and her car. They were halfway down the steps when she stopped short and her hand went to her throat. The man who blocked their way looked gigantic in the fading sunlight. He loomed above them, his shoulders hunched, his pale white face impassive.

"It's all right, Kirsten," Jake said quickly. "This is Murray." His voice was gentle as he spoke to the man.

Murray's still face turned toward Kirsten. He had hooded eyes and an empty expression. Then he looked, slowly, at Jake. "For a ride?"

"Yes. It's a beautiful night."

Murray looked once again at Kirsten, looked long and hard.

Kirsten tensed. What was he thinking and why did he stare at her so hard?

"You'll be careful." The tone was wooden, monotonous.

"Sure we will, Murray." Jake smiled, patted the man once again on the arm, and then urged Kirsten on down the steps.

All the way to the car, Kirsten was aware of the silent figure standing on the steps, staring down at them.

As Jake slipped behind the wheel she looked back and said abruptly, "He's still watching us."

"Hey, Kirsten, relax." Jake's tone was easy. "It really is all right. Murray wouldn't hurt a soul."

"But who is he?" she asked sharply.

"Murray is …" Jake paused and shook his head a little. "It's a long story, Kirsten, and not a happy one. I was a lieutenant in Vietnam, and I wouldn't be standing on this deck right now if it weren't for Murray. Someday I'll tell you all about it, but not tonight."

He drove fast, one arm around her. When they reached the marina he held tightly to her hand as they boarded the cruiser. Once the cruiser was underway, he turned and looked at her and his eyes were luminous in the dark. Neither of them spoke, but there was a sense of wonder between them, an expectancy that needed no words. When they were out of sight of land, he slowed the cruiser to a stop, then turned and reached out to her.

She moved slowly into his arms and welcomed the pressure of his body against hers. She looked up into his dark eyes, eyes full of love and desire. He smiled down at her, then one hand touched her cheek. She turned her face to kiss his palm, then his hands cupped her face and his mouth found hers. They kissed, a long, slow, sweet and gentle kiss, one, then another, and another.

His hand tangled in her hair. "You are so incredibly lovely," he said, his voice deep and soft. "Kirsten, Kirsten."

She pressed the palms of her hands against his back, thrilling to the hard, solid feel of his muscles. "I thought you were going to take me home early."

He laughed. "I may never take you home."

He picked her up then and began to walk across the deck and she knew he was going to the master cabin where she'd changed that first day. She knew that now was the time to slip free. She had never loved any man but Aubrey, and that after a long and ardent courtship. She had never imagined that any man could captivate her so quickly, so absolutely. She knew that if she didn't stop now she would not stop.

She awoke first and didn't know for a moment where she was. Then she did know and she felt a sense of wonder. Raising up on her elbow, she looked down at Jake as he slept and felt a rush of love and affection and happiness. She'd always discounted those old tales of love at first sight, but now she knew they could be true, that there could be an instant understanding and knowledge between two people. Shirley MacLaine would insist they'd known each other in another life. She tried to picture Jake in other times. Yes, he would have made a wonderful Roman soldier or Spanish conquistador. But not, and her grin widened, a Puritan. Or she either, for heaven's sake.

His eyes opened. He looked up, sleepily, then quizzically.

"I'm not sure whether to be pleased or worried when I wake up and find a beautiful woman laughing at me."

"Actually, I was trying to envision you as a Puritan and not having any success."

"A Puritan," he mused. Then he grinned, too. "Whatever put that in your mind?"

And it was delightful, when she told him, that he understood at once and quickly said she would have been a marvelous Viking maid or perhaps a headstrong Elizabethan.

He bunched a pillow behind his head. "What a wonderful way to wake up. This morning I almost believe I know what it is to be Irish."

"Irish?"

"You know how the Irish are. Three miracles before breakfast and a leprechaun for afternoon tea wouldn't faze them at all." He reached out and stroked her hair. "One miracle before breakfast is more than I ever expected."

Kirsten studied him soberly. "No one's ever called me a miracle before."

"The more fool they," he said. His hand traced the line of her face, then cupped her chin. Slowly, he drew her down to him. "Oh, Kirsten."

They loved each other.

She kissed his face, tiny, brushing kisses that slipped across his bristly cheek and to his ear and down his throat to his chest, and she pressed her face against the wiry mat of hair.

His hands caressed her, lightly, lovingly, lingeringly. There was no hurry, no pressure. They had all the day and all the world to love in, and they knew it and took their time and their pleasure, delighting in each other and the perfection of the moment. When the pulse of desire began to race, their lips met and they moved together, sharing the exquisite, breathtaking explosion of passion.

When they lay quietly in each other's arms, Kirsten wished the moment would never end. Here, together on the ocean, they were free of the outside world and all its dangers and problems. She felt a sudden coldness. One day she would have to tell Jake how they'd met. And what would he do then?

7

THEY HAD TWO WONDERFUL days. Later, Kirsten would remember them with an ache in her heart. She should have known to be frightened. When life is perfect, that is when the gods are jealous and heartbreak lies in store. It wasn't, of course, a supernatural power that destroyed her future, hers and Jake Johnson's.

Tuesday was the first perfect day, beginning with her early morning sail through the patches of fog and Jake's welcome to the cruiser.

Wednesday was the second perfect day, beginning with their slow and languorous lovemaking and their laughter over conquistadores and Viking maids. After a lunch of cold Chablis and a Caesar salad on the afterdeck, Jake ruefully shook his head.

"Do you know why I came to California?"

"Why?"

"Because there are so many distractions in Washington and New York."

"Are you trying to tell me something?" she asked.

He took her hand and held it tightly. "No. I'm trying to tell myself something. I do have work that can't wait. Do you mind?"

Kirsten stretched like a lazy cat. "No. I don't mind at all. Besides, I should get back to my room, I need to work, too."

He looked at her admiringly. "You are remarkable."

Surprised, she asked, "What's remarkable about that?"

"Most women I've known," and there was a bitter tone in his voice, "are unalterably opposed to a man devoting time to anything or anyone but them."

"Perhaps you've know the wrong women," she said mildly.

"There's no doubt about that." Again, his tone was almost harsh. He stared off across the water, but she knew he wasn't seeing the ocean. Then, with a visible effort, he smiled. "You really are marvelous, Kirsten – and you aren't an actress."

So there it was and now she knew the report she'd read was accurate, at least so far as his feelings about actresses were concerned. She didn't want to ask, but she had to.

"Why don't you like actresses, Jake?"

He turned back to her and there was no lightness in his face now. He looked tired and drained. "I was married once, Kirsten."

She waited.

"Francesca …" He paused.

Kirsten felt a sudden emptiness. Did he still care? Was Francesca Montez still so important to him?

"Francesca never knows what's real and what isn't," he continued. "But she's always center stage. She has to be, and she can't understand that a man has responsibilities, that there are times, many times, when he can't dance attendance." His mouth curved in a wry smile. "That's exactly what Francesca expects – for everyone to dance attendance upon her." He shrugged. "But I should have known better. Actresses can't help but be vain and self-centered. It goes with the territory. And they can't help acting – all the time."

Kirsten, too, looked out across the water, and, mixed with the pain of knowing that Jake obviously was still emotionally involved with his memories of Francesca, was a feeling of kinship.

"I was married once, too," she said quietly.

He waited and she was grateful for the questions he didn't ask.

"It didn't last long." Sudden hot tears stung her eyes and she tried to will them away. She bit her lip. "I grew up thinking marriage was forever. I knew mine would be. I had no doubts about it."

Jake still held her hand and he gave it a quick squeeze. "Did you love him so much?" and now his eyes were dark with pain.

"That's the worst part," she said slowly. "I thought I did. I truly thought I did – and then I found out that I didn't know him at all, that everything I imagined him to be was just that – imagination." She paused, then said reluctantly, "Aubrey is an actor, and when I look back I see that he was playing a part with me. He was a young man in love." She looked at Jake. "It sounds like the title of a play." The brittle note in her voice gave way to uncertainty. "Ever since then, I haven't trusted myself or my judgments. If I could be so wrong about Aubrey … "

"How did it go wrong?"

Kirsten stared at him for a long moment. How did it go wrong? How did that marriage that was meant to last a lifetime turn into a nightmare of unhappiness?

"I'll always wonder why he married me."

Jake said quickly, "That's easy enough to understand."

"I was working for an agent and I met Aubrey at a cocktail party. Sometimes I think he just dated me to have a chance to meet Mr. Faber. He was the agent. But why did Aubrey marry me?" Once again, the tears smarted in her eyes.

Jake pulled her close to him on the wicker sofa. "Hey, Kirsten, take it easy. He married you because you are beautiful and wonderful."

"Three weeks after we were married, I came back to our apartment unexpectedly – and Aubrey was there with Monique Morris, who had the lead in the play he was trying out for."

She didn't have to tell Jake how she'd found them.

"What a goddamned fool," Jake said explosively.

She managed a smile at that. "You're nice," she said suddenly. "You're very nice." Then her smile faded and she looked uncertain, defeated. "You can't imagine how devastating it is to realize your husband prefers a woman twenty years older than you are – and then to realize you married a man you didn't love – and who didn't love you." She took a deep breath. "So that's the story of a very short marriage and a woman who decided she wasn't ever going to trust another man."

"Do you still feel that way?" he asked quietly.

"I don't know how I feel." Then she said quickly, "Oh, yes I do. I know very well how I feel. I've fallen for you in a very big way and it's not something I expected – or wanted. I'd built a very nice shell – and now it's ruptured and I don't know what's going to happen to me."

"I had a shell, too," he said slowly. "But life in a shell isn't very satisfactory is it?"

"No."

He heard the tremor in her voice. "I promise you, Kirsten, I won't ever hurt you," and he pulled her close and held her tight.

Kirsten clung to him and felt tears squeeze from her closed eyelids. That was his promise, but what would happen one day when she told him all the truth about herself?

Jake flipped rapidly through the first folder until he found the section on current availability of air-to-air weapons of medium range. He paused and put on his wire-rim reading glasses and settled down for a thorough study. He was frowning before he reached the end of the first page. If the production delays of the new AIM-120 continued, it was going to leave U.S. defenses woefully weakened. Why the hell couldn't the armament industry meet production schedules? He pulled a legal pad closer and began to write. He paused at the end of the page and, suddenly, with no warning, he wasn't looking at the densely packed pages of typescript, he was seeing Kirsten's face, the deep-set, blue eyes, the delicately chiseled, aristocratic features which could look so aloof and distant, but he had seen a Kirsten so far removed from that public image, her eyes soft with desire, her mouth open, her lips seeking.

He stared unseeingly at the legal pad. He felt a lightness of spirit that he hadn't experienced in years. He felt young and alive and eager for love. Funny. He'd had women, many of them. Some he'd liked, others he'd admired, many he'd just desired, but no faces remained with him and he didn't care if he ever saw any of them again. But Kirsten … It wasn't her youth or even her beauty, it was the magic of her being, the sense of completion he felt when he was with her. He'd told her that now he almost understood what it was to be Irish and to expect a miracle before breakfast. Could he also expect that greatest of all miracles, a lasting love? He pushed the papers aside and reached for the telephone.

Kirsten stopped at the Carmel Gate to the 17-Mile Drive and called out, "I'm Kirsten Soderstrom and I'm expected at the Johnson house."

The attendant waved her through. She put the red Porsche into gear and roared off. When she reported to the FBI agent and told him they were all wrong about Jake, she was going to miss the Porsche. She grinned and gunned around a curve, delighting in the wind streaming through her hair and the glimpses of ocean far below, and the colorful, magnificent, sun shining on the water.

Success was to be part of her cover, of course, her presentation of herself to Jake as a wealthy young woman with ample funds to spend the summer writing a book in Carmel. So far, Jake hadn't commented on the car. She slowed down for an especially tricky curve. She frowned. She hoped she wouldn't have to tell him about the investigation. Would Ellis Kemp agree to that? Let her return the car and shake free of the undercover operation? Surely, he would.

Ellis Kemp had such cold eyes. Kirsten nervously beat a tattoo on the steering wheel. Every time she thought about him she felt half sick. She'd been so relieved when she went back to her apartment in the afternoon and found no message from him. She knew the message would come, one day or another, the message giving her instructions to make her search at the Johnson house and when to meet her contact with a report. But at least there had been no message this afternoon and she was free to do what she wished, and what she wished to do … She laughed aloud. It was a good thing Jake couldn't read her mind. Would he be shocked at her thoughts when they were talking on the phone and he invited her to the house for dinner? She wasn't thinking about her script or his work or the investigation. She was thinking how they might sail after dinner, and when they were alone perhaps they would dance and she would be in his arms and then …

They had cocktails on the terrace overlooking the ocean. It was an easy, relaxed group and the conversation ranged from the absurd (how to name a frog in the Calaveras Jumping Frog Jubilee) to the serious (the prospects for peace in Latin America), but Kirsten was marveling at her control and Jake's. No one would suppose they were lovers from their manner. Although they sat side by side on a wicker couch there was a decorous distance between them. They schooled their faces, expressing pleasure and, of course, interest, but the soft glances they'd shared were absent. Once or twice, their eyes met and held for just an instant and each knew the other's thoughts but no one else would know. Kirsten controlled the happiness that pounded within her with as much force and pressure as the booming surf that crashed into the black, basalt rocks so far below.

Happy, happy, happy, what a marvelously happy day. It was at that instant of feeling that a small quiver of unease struck her. If she and Jake could mask their feelings so well, then what about Amy and Drew, who were laughing and gesturing and were so perfectly a part of this civilized scene?

Because someone had informed Ellis Kemp that Jake was coming to California. The list was short, Mrs. Johnson, Amy, Drew, and Murray. Murray – she must find out more about him. He seemed such a sinister figure but obviously Jake didn't think so.

Jake and Drew were deep into a discussion of the Contras in Nicaragua.

Kirsten turned to Amy. "How did you happen to go to work for Jake?"

Once again, there was a sensation of strain, the same feeling she'd sensed at her first dinner at the Johnson home. Kirsten kept the look of polite inquiry on her face but inside she churned with questions. Was there an old romance here? How could such an innocuous question cause the look of distress on Amy's face?

Amy's almond-shaped eyes widened. She paused for a long moment, then said briefly, "My husband was a close friend of Jake's."

Curiouser and curiouser. There'd been no mention of Amy's husband, but before Kirsten could ask, Amy continued in a controlled, even tone.

"I'm a widow." Briskly, she asked, "Are you married?"

Kirsten sat very still. It was turnabout fair play, wasn't it? "Not now."

They smiled warily at each other and their talk slipped into a discussion of the new fashions.

"Have you seen any of those bag dresses?" Amy asked.

Jake picked up on that and they decided that after dinner they'd take a pile of trash sacks and some cellophane and, of course, a hefty swath of aluminum foil and see what they could come up with. They were all laughing as they walked into the dining room. Mrs. Johnson came down the stairs to join them and smiled at their laughter.

Kirsten studied Drew during a delicious dinner. Roast lamb with mint jelly, snow peas, and new potatoes.

Drew appeared more at ease and at home than Jake who several times seemed abstracted. Drew described how he'd persuaded a Carmel gallery-owner to let him bring a Degas out to the house. "I pointed out to him that no one could make that kind of purchase without being certain the picture was right for the room."

Amy laughed. "Drew, you're crazy. What room wouldn't be right for a De-gas?"

Drew laughed. "The gallery owner's an ass. I couldn't resist it."

Jake looked puzzled. "What's the point?"

Drew shrugged. "Who knows? I might actually buy it. It would look great in my apartment."

"It would look better in a museum," Amy objected.

Drew shot a glance at the Turner hanging above the mantel across from the table. "So you object to private acquisition of art works?"

"Oh no," she stammered. "Not at all." Then she said quickly, "You're just kidding anyway. You can't afford a Degas."

"There's where you're wrong," he drawled. "I took a flyer on the ponies last week and won the double. I can too afford a Degas. At least, one Degas."

Jake laughed. "Then buy it, Drew."

They finished dinner and decided against dessert, then Jake was pulling back her chair and generally addressing the room, "Would anyone like to go out for a cruise? It's a great night."

Mrs. Johnson smiled and shook her head.

Drew pulled out an after-dinner cigar. "I'll opt for the terrace, thanks. A Degas, yes. A yacht, no."

Jake grinned. "Anyone who can smoke cigars should be able to go out in a boat."

Amy smiled and declined, too, and Jake and Kirsten walked across the ter-race toward the steps and the path to the drive.

When they reached the Porsche, Kirsten took the wheel this time and asked, "Did you expect anyone to come with us?"

"Absolutely not. I don't pay people to be stupid."

She laughed at that. "They seem nice," she said impulsively. "Both of them."

"I couldn't make it without them."

"Tell me about Amy and Drew," she said as she curved the Porsche down the drive.

Jake looked toward the setting sun which hung like a ball of molten fire just above the horizon.

"Amy." He said her name quietly. Then he shook his head. "Some people don't have many breaks." His voice was quiet, subdued when he spoke again. "Amy and I go back a long way."

Kirsten swallowed. Perhaps she shouldn't have asked. Sometimes it was better not to know.

"I met her at a beach party when I was at Berkeley and I thought she was a really nice girl so I made a point of getting her together with my roommate, Bill Montgomery."

The squeeze around Kirsten's heart began to ease. This was a love story, but not Jake's love story.

"They fell in love?"

"It should have been a happily-ever-after story. But this was 1968 and a lot of love stories ended like theirs. Bill was killed when he was leading a patrol in Nam and he stepped on a Claymore mine." Jake's face was somber in the bright glow of the setting sun, somber and grim. "He was twenty-three years old and he and Amy would have celebrated their first anniversary the next day."

"You were in Vietnam, too. That's where you met Murray."

Jake nodded, then smiled wryly. "A lot of my life is tied up in those years. It's something that happened to a lot of us and you can't forget it, not even if you want to. It changed the way we looked at life and our country. That's why I got into politics when I got back." He looked down at Kirsten. "You're so young," he said gently. "I don't know if you can ever understand that part of me."

"I want to understand. I want to understand very much."

Slowly he nodded.

"Tell me about Murray."

"Murray's younger than I am."

Kirsten stared at him in disbelief, recalling Murray's drawn pale face and hunched figure.

"I led a platoon, and Murray was my sergeant. He was just a big kid out of Iowa, but he knew a lot more Army that I ever learned. We were three days from the end of our tour – three days – and we were on a helicopter that caught a burst of flak and went down. I was crammed between a side gun turret and a seat, but somehow Murray pulled the stuff away and dragged me out. He carried me about fifty yards downhill, then ran back for some others. The copter blew up just before he reached it. Murray never quite came back from it."

"You've taken care of him ever since," she said gently.

"Oh no," he said quickly. "Murray takes care of me. You'll see."

His calm assumption that she would become a part of his life filled her with a sense of warmth and security that she hadn't felt in years, perhaps had never felt. She'd been seven when her mother died and she carried with her the legacy of that loss, a sense of impermanence and understanding that all life is change, that nothing lasts forever.

To be a part of Jake's life – again she felt the dark edge of concern because there was something hidden in his life of which he was unaware, but perhaps she could help him without having to reveal herself. She needed to know everything she could about the people around him.

When they boarded the cruiser and were well underway, she asked, "Was Drew in Vietnam, too?"

Jake's face lightened and he smiled. "No. Drew has a talent for avoiding the unpleasant. Actually, I think he was a 4-F."

"Has he been with you as long as Amy and Murray?"

"All my life. Drew's my cousin."

That explained a lot. No wonder Drew could talk so easily about buying paintings by Degas and looked so at ease in luxurious surroundings.

"But he does me a heck of a job. I'm grateful he's satisfied to work for me. He could have a big time PR firm of his own if he wanted. He knows how to handle the press and get the most out of every story. Drew's no fool even if he likes to act like one."

The widow of his college roommate, the man who saved his life in Vietnam and his cousin who wasn't a fool – Kirsten felt totally discouraged. It didn't make sense. Maybe she was off on the wrong track altogether. But someone had informed the FBI that Jake was coming to California. He came at the last minute, a secret decision. Everyone else on his staff thought he was in New York, so there had to be an enemy in that very small circle around him. The widow of his college roommate, the man who saved his life in Vietnam, his cousin who wasn't a fool. Was there more to one of them that Jake – or anyone else – realized?

The cruiser rocked slowly in a swell.

"Why so somber?" he asked quietly, reaching out to take her hand.

Kirsten looked up and wanted to erase the concern from his eyes. He had such a strong face with its sharp angles and blunt chin, but she could see more than strength. She could see gentleness and compassion and a willingness to meet life on whatever terms it offered, from the worst to the best, to meet any challenge with courage and good humor and a very special grace of spirit which refuses to accept the second-rate or the shoddy. She felt a blinding flash of anger at whoever was trying to enmesh him in a scandal, trying to destroy this fine and good man.

"I want you to know," she said slowly, "that I care very much for you." She smiled tremulously. "I love you."

He was quiet for a long moment, staring down at her, his dark eyes searching hers, then he pulled her into his arms and his mouth was soft against her hair. "And now a miracle after dinner," he whispered. "Kirsten, I love you, too."

They stood in the circle of each other's arms and spoke of love and time and tomorrow and all the tomorrows that could come.

He carried her to the cabin and when they were lying together they caressed each other and gave and took pleasure. Then there was no more thought, only feeling, and the joy of loving and being loved, and a sense of shared wonder that she could understand and be understood to the depth of her being, a mystic communication that transcended the physical.

When they rested, she looked up into his warm, dark, loving eyes and made a promise, though, of course, he didn't know it. She would do the right thing for him. Whatever it was.

That was the end of the second perfect day.

8

"I TOLD YOU THE Senator liked blondes."

The paunchy man lounged behind the battered desk in the flimsy two-room office that overlooked a squalid assortment of used cars in a lot on La Brea. He rarely had customers and didn't spend much time at his businessbut there was no one to care or to notice that a few people seemed to return and take time looking at cars, but they never bought. He shifted his cold cigar from one corner of his mouth to the other and spoke in his high, soft voice into the telephone receiver. "So he's hooked?"

"Line and sinker."

The heavy man didn't answer for a moment. Even after all these years, he had trouble with idioms, though he spoke English with no accent. "Are the papers there?" he asked.

"Yes, and my end's already taken care of."

"So now it's up to the girl."

"Right. That's why I called." Impatience edged the voice. "Have you sent her the key and her instructions?"

"They were placed in her apartment yesterday evening right after she left."

The caller laughed. "I'll say he's hooked. She must have spent the night on the yacht. Well, that's all right. She'll find the stuff this afternoon. How long did you give her?"

"Until Saturday."

There was a pause. "What happens after Saturday?"

The paunchy man laid the cold cigar in a ceramic ashtray. "I wouldn't worry about that if I were you."

Kirsten licked her lips and stared down at the small key in the palm of her hand. She'd known the moment was coming, but somehow, in the delight of the last two days, she'd pushed that expectation deep inside. Now, she couldn't ignore any longer why she was in Carmel and all the puzzling, inexplicable things she'd learned. Most importantly, and no one would ever convince her otherwise, she'd learned that Jake Johnson was an honorable man and that deceit wasn't part of his nature. She couldn't prove that in a court of law, but she knew it in her heart and that was the most demanding tribunal of all, so now she had to decide how best to meet the challenge to his integrity.

Should she go to the house now, this moment, and tell him about it from the very first and let him confront the FBI? Her instructions said tersely that the bribe money was in his study safe, $50,000.

If she told Jake, it would, of course, open her to attack from the FBI. She shrugged that away. What would be best for Jake? The FBI could claim that she'd warned him, given him an opportunity to do away with damaging evidence. That would be true, of course, if he were guilty. She knew he wasn't, but there would always be a question if she told him of the investigation. On the other hand, if she searched for the money, followed the instructions so neatly typed out on the paper lying on the table, then she could prove no money was there. She would have photographs of an empty safe and her own testimony.

Kirsten took a deep breath and looked once again at the small gold key.

Jake balanced at the end of the high board.

Kirsten shaded her eyes from the sun and looked up. She kept her face carefully free of expression but she felt a throb of desire. He was so magnificent, his broad chest and superbly-muscled legs tensed for the dive. No one ever looked better.

"Jake tells me you want to be a scriptwriter," Drew said.

Kirsten turned to him. Drew was lying back on a soft vinyl chair, hands propped behind his head. He looked as comfortable and good-humored as a teddy bear. She managed a smile, though she would much rather have continued to watch Jake. Then she heard the smooth splash and knew she'd missed Jake's dive. Damn Drew. But she managed to speak pleasantly.

"Yes, but I know what the odds are."

"Jake can probably help you."

Drew had light blue eyes, very pale blue eyes. She realized he was watching her closely.

"I wouldn't expect that."

Drew shrugged. "You'd better take a hand up where you can get it. That's how the world works, and especially in Hollywood."

Kirsten knew that was true and knew that introductions and recommendations were just that and nothing more; that in the final analysis whatever you did had to stand on its own merit, but she didn't want ever to ask Jake to help her.

Then Jake was sprinkling water on her from the pool. "Come on in. The water's fine."

Kirsten stood and began to slip out of her robe – and loved the look in Jake's eyes. Then, reluctantly, she paused. "Jake, I'm supposed to call Mr. Faber's office this afternoon. Do you mind if I run in the house and call? Then I'll swim with you."

"Of course. You know the way."

She smiled, a bright, cheerful smile, but her heart was thumping. She pulled the robe back on and turned to cross the terrace. As she pulled open the French door, she accounted for everyone in her mind. It was midafternoon and Mrs. Johnson was resting in her room. Already Kirsten was learning the pulse of the house. Jake and Drew were by the pool. Amy Montgomery had gone into Carmel and she could see Murray washing a car near the garages. That left only the servants.

Kirsten walked faster and felt the heaviness in her right robe pocket. She slipped her hand into the pocket and felt the cold metal of the camera that looked like a compact. Her left hand dropped into the other pocket and closed around the key to the safe.

Once inside the study she looked swiftly around. Good. The curtains were drawn so all she had to fear was an unexpected entrance from the hall door. She hurried across the room to the desk and, yes, just as her instructions had indicated, there was a wooden cabinet on the wall. She pulled it open then looked uneasily over her shoulder. Her heart pounded erratically. She felt a wave of nausea. Nothing had ever prepared her for the task of poking into private places with absolutely no hope of satisfactorily explaining her actions should she be discovered. Her hands shook as she took the small yellow key and inserted it in the safe lock. It turned smoothly and she pulled open the safe then, once again, glanced over her shoulder. She was breathing fast as if she had run a long distance, and there was a film of sweat on her hands. Quickly, she yanked out the compact and turned it on its side, then moved the tiny decorative scroll that masked the lens. She turned back to the safe and, for a moment, her heart stopped. There was something in the safe. She laid down the camera, reached into the safe and pulled out the materials and saw, stamped on the cover of the two blue manila folders, TOP SECRET-CONFIDENTIAL. She shook the folders, then peered into the back of the shallow safe. She began to smile. There wasn't anything else in the safe, nothing at all, and certainly not $50,000. She snatched up the camera and photographed the interior of the safe several times until she was certain she had it from every angle and the photos would show that only the folders were there. Quickly, quickly, she closed and locked the safe, then shut the cabinet and turned back to lean against the desk as drained as though she'd run a race. She dropped the camera in one pocket and the key in the other and looked around the room in triumph. She'd done it, she'd done it all, completed the assignment and proved conclusively that Jake wasn't a crook.

She was scheduled to meet her contact in San Francisco Saturday afternoon. This was Thursday afternoon. That meant no action would be taken on her information before Monday at the earliest and who knew how long it would take and what channels information such as hers must travel. No, that was too long, and, besides, she didn't like this faceless reporting. She needed to talk to the FBI agent in person and make him understand that there was a mistake somewhere, that their information concerning Jake was wrong, dead wrong.

She reached out and picked up the phone and dialed information. When she had the FBI number in Los Angeles, she hesitated for a moment, but her dad always said, go to the top man. She dialed and asked for Ellis Kemp and was put on hold. Then, just as a voice came on the line, Jake walked into the study.

Kirsten stood frozen for an instant, then she said brightly, "Yes, tell him Kirsten Soderstrom called – and I'll be in town early tomorrow morning to talk to him." Then, shielding the phone from Jake's view with her body, she depressed the cradle bar and continued, "I'm very excited and I'll have a synopsis with me. Yes. Thanks so much." She hung up the phone, then turned to Jake, beaming. "I've got the best news. Mr. Faber left word that he has a director interested in my script idea and he's set up a lunch tomorrow at the Beverly Wilshire."

"That calls for a celebration." He picked her up and swung her around and Kirsten was terribly conscious of the camera in one pocket and the safe key in the other. Then he let her down slowly, very slowly, and held her softly against him. She felt the warmth of his body and the smooth hard muscles of his chest and legs, and the desire that had flickered earlier flamed within her – and he knew it.

"I know the finest way to celebrate," he said urgently.

"Jake, not here. We can't …"

He held her tightly for an instant more, then took her hand and pulled her with him. "We'll take a walk."

"A walk?" For heaven's sake, what did he have in mind?

He grinned at her as they hurried down the hall. "You haven't seen all of the grounds."

She stretched her legs to keep up with his long stride. "Jake Johnson," she said sharply, "I will admit that I am besotted over you, but there are limits, distinct limits, and one of those includes making love in public places."

He paused and looked down at her with a small grin, a very satisfied grin. "I'll bet I could change your mind."

She didn't want to laugh. That would encourage him and he certainly didn't need any encouragement, but she did laugh. "Funny thing is," she replied, "I don't bet."

They turned and crossed the terrace and Drew looked up at them sharply.

Jake waved. "I'm going to show Kirsten the summerhouse. She won't believe me when I tell her we have white-tailed deer."

Drew subsided sleepily on his deck chair. "What energy. Say hello to the deer for me."

They took a path that angled to the side of the house and then toward the back and Kirsten exclaimed, "I've never seen a lovelier garden."

The house, a long rambling Mediterranean style villa, stretched along the top of a wooded rise overlooking the Pacific. Kirsten had sat on the terrace and seen the magnificent view of the sharply-shelving cliff and rugged rocks of the coastline and the endless variation in the mood and sweep of the water as it thundered to shore, but she hadn't seen the wooded hillside behind the house with its beds of flaming gladiolas and elegant irises bounded by the dark and twisted cypresses with their aromatic scent and the towering pines.

Tucked between two enormous pines at the base of the hillside was a gazebo. Kirsten realized it would have a magnificent view, because it was higher than the house. It was open to the breeze and yet it would, she knew, be very private, very isolated. They would be absolutely alone.

Kirsten looked up at Jake and she knew what her eyes revealed. She felt a thrill of excitement compounded of desire and triumph; she was going to prove Jake's innocence, and a wild elation with herself and him and the moment. She grinned up at him. "Catch me if you can," and she turned and began to run, the long, easy stride she'd perfected as a cross-country runner in school – and that would show him he didn't know everything there was to know about her.

"Hey," he called out in surprise, then she heard him running, too, heard the steady drum of his feet and felt a little surprise of her own as he came even then she gave it a kick and spurted ahead, but, once again he was closing the gap and they came up hard against the gazebo steps and she was in his arms and they struggled for breath as they laughed and clung to each other.

"Damn good," he gasped. "Track team?"

She nodded and drew gulps of air into her aching chest. "Pretty good yourself." Then as her breathing evened out and she became more aware of him and the feel of his body against hers, she said softly, pressing her hands against his back, "Hmm, hmm, good."

They turned together and walked up the steps into the gazebo and spread a long mat from a wicker couch onto the wooden floor. They began slowly and then passion surged and they moved together explosively, wildly, triumphantly.

Jake propped up on an elbow and looked down at her appreciatively. "You are wonderful."

Kirsten reached up and touched his lips. "Because of you."

70

"Let's see," he mused. "On a boat. In a gazebo. Hey listen, I've got an airplane. If we put the plane on automatic pilot …"

She quirked an eyebrow. "Will you still love me in an ordinary room?"

"Oh, yes. I'll love you in the air, on the ground, under water. Anywhere. Everywhere. Day. Night. Rain or shine."

Her smile slipped away. "No matter what happens in the future?"

"No matter what."

Amy Montgomery stood at the corner of Sixth and Mission and waited for the light to change. A red Porsche roared past. The light changed but Amy Montgomery stood unmoving, staring after the bright red sports car and its beautiful blonde driver. Amy's hands tightened on her shopping bag. Some people had all the luck, didn't they? She swallowed. Someone nudged her from behind and she realized the light had changed and she started across the street. She and Bill … Bill had been dead so long, so very long, and, in all that time, she'd had no one to love, no one to love her. She paused and stared into a shop window. Sometimes she hated Jake Johnson, hated him for being alive while Bill was dead. She took a deep breath and turned and moved on, walking fast.

Kirsten paused at the base of the broad, white stone steps. She'd rehearsed what she was going to say all the way down the coast in the bumpy commuter flight, but now that the moment had come she felt a wave of panic. This was so important, so vitally important. She had to do it right, be properly persuasive, convince Ellis Kemp that the sting operation against Jake was wrong, that he wasn't taking money, that any wrongdoing must be the act of a staff member without Jake's knowledge. That could be, of course. She hurried up the steps and pushed through the main entrance. It happened all the time. Well, if not all the time, certainly it had happened before. Someone in a position of influence with a powerful official would accept money, presumably on behalf of the official but, in actuality, to enrich themselves. Usually, it was done when the person accepting the money knew the official's position on a matter would profit a company. That could be how the whole thing started – and Jake wouldn't even be aware of it.

She paused in the lobby and found the floor and office number and waited for the elevator. All the way to the third floor she arranged her facts in her mind and tried not to think of the implications of what she would tell Kemp, but her mind pulled at the problem. What staff member? She felt a moment of utter confusion. Could one staff member be working with the FBI, informing them when Jake would be in California so that Kirsten could make her advance? But that would mean one staff member was with the FBI and another was the cause of the problem, if Kirsten were right in her appraisal, and, really, that didn't make sense.

She held hard to one clear fact. She hadn't found any money in Jake's safe, so that knocked the FBI theory into a cocked hat, didn't it? Of course, it did.

She paused outside the frosted door, took another deep breath, then opened it and stepped inside. The receptionist took her name and asked her to wait. Kirsten sat on the edge of the hard wooden chair, then forced herself to sit back and relax. If she'd ever needed to be in control, this was the time.

The receptionist looked up and smiled. "Mr. Kemp will see you now. He's the third office on the right."

Kirsten pushed through the wooden railing and turned down the long hallway. She felt suddenly at home. These offices smelled so much the way her father's had, a mixture of tobacco smoke and closed-in air and dust and old wooden furniture. She was smiling as she stopped in the open doorway of the third office.

The man behind the desk looked up, then his eyes brightened and he rose.

Kirsten reached out and gripped the doorjamb. This was the third office. The nameplate on the desk said ELLIS KEMP – and she'd never in all her life seen the tall, thin man standing behind the desk.

"Are you all right?" The man spoke in a quick, clipped New York accent. He stared at her in concern and started around the desk.

"Ellis Kemp?" Her voice was thin, high, rising.

He stopped and stared at her, frowning. "Yes, I'm Ellis Kemp."

She began to shake her head. "No." She stepped back a pace. "No, you can't be."

He looked at her warily. "Lady, my name is Ellis Kemp. Now, what can I do for you?"

Kirsten stared at him for a long moment and panic welled up in her mind, swept through her. The man she'd called Ellis Kemp, who was he? Whoever he was, he wasn't an FBI agent, and that meant the FBI wasn't investigating Jake Johnson, and that meant ....

The agent took a step toward her.

She was involved in something dark and dangerous, but she had no way of proving her story. This man would question her sanity if she burst out with a story of a casting agency and an FBI agent and a sting operation ... She watched the agent approach, then swung around and hurried down the hall and pushed through the gate. She ran to the hall door and opened it.

Ellis Kemp moved quickly, but when he stood in the doorway and looked down the hall there was no trace of the beautiful blonde. He frowned then turned back and shrugged his shoulders and spoke to the receptionist. "You sure get all kinds – but she was awfully pretty to be a nut."

9

SMOG HUNG THICK AND yellow over the Los Angeles basin. Kirsten's eyes burned even though the air conditioning hummed in the rental car. She drove too fast, cutting across lanes of traffic, and after she parked she almost ran up the sidewalk to the building entrance. She did run up the stairs to the second floor, but she needn't have bothered. The door to the casting agency was closed and locked and a *For Rent* placard hung crookedly from the doorknob. She stood in the dusty, quiet hall and stared at the locked door.

There was no casting agency, of course. She'd known that. She'd accepted the word of the man who called himself Ellis Kemp that he was an FB I agent looking for an actress to help in a sting operation against a corrupt senator. He wasn't Ellis Kemp. There was no sting operation.

What was she involved in?

Kirsten remembered the heavy-set man's eyes, cold eyes, eyes that seemed both empty and dangerous.

She was involved in some kind of conspiracy, a conspiracy with Jake Johnson as its target. Kirsten reached out and grabbed the doorknob and rattled it. The metallic sound twanged against the silence of the hallway but the door didn't move and no one came.

Oh Jake, Jake, what had she done?

Kirsten felt a wash of panic just as if an enormous breaker towered over her, poised to crash down and fling her helplessly to the ocean floor. She clung to the doorknob and tried to quiet her breathing. She had to be calm. She had to think and act, purposefully, cleverly, intelligently. If ever in her life it mattered that she do the right thing, it was now. Jake Johnson's future depended upon her. She had brought danger to him, but now if she did the right thing perhaps she could divert and defuse that danger. Only she knew that a conspiracy threatened.

She didn't know the purpose of the conspiracy. Could she find out? Who was behind it? What was the goal? Why did it target Jake Johnson?

She turned and hurried downstairs and found the building manager's office. She inquired for the forwarding address of the casting agency.

She looked worriedly at the bent-shouldered manager. "They got away owing me a check for two months' work."

He didn't move for a long moment, then, wearily, boredly, he pulled open a filing cabinet. Finally, he looked up. "Nope. Don't have a new address. Just a post office box number."

Kirsten didn't try to hide her disappointment.

The manager shrugged. "Yeah, that's no help, is it? They just won't answer your letter." The man hesitated then said slyly, "I might be able to give you a hand."

Kirsten waited.

"Course, you know, it could mean my job."

Kirsten understood. "I could give you twenty dollars."

He took the money and tucked it in the waistband of his jeans then said softly, "I got the license numbers of two different cars that parked in the slot for that office. You never know when information is going to come in handy."

Kirsten knew this wasn't the first time he'd made a buck with pieces of information.

"One car was a brown Ford Falcon, a '79, and the other was a little red Fiat, about an '82."

Kirsten wrote down the license numbers, but that didn't account for the excited thudding of her heart. A little red Fiat – one of the cars at the Johnson house was a little red Fiat— so what were the odds the license plates matched?

"Did you notice anything else interesting?"

The manager shook his head, then said suddenly, "The guy who rented the offices – I didn't like his eyes."

The commuter flight going north was just as bumpy as the one she'd taken south that morning, but Kirsten was oblivious to the erratic lurches. Questions circled frantically in her mind. Okay, since she wasn't involved in a sting, then what was the man's reason to hire her? There had to be a reason and it had to be a big reason to make it worth the money they' paid her, plus the use of a Porsche. The Porsche … Maybe it could be traced. Then her shoulders slumped a little. No. It would turn out to be a stolen car or some other kind of dead end. There was no chance it would be registered nicely in the real name of the man behind the scheme.

Of course, they had no idea she'd tumbled to the existence of a conspiracy. So far as they knew she was still the gull, the dupe, the patsy.

They … she kept calling the man and whoever he really worked for 'they,' and what did she mean? Somehow, she had to find out who these people were. Perhaps that would give her some inkling what they intended and why they'd hired her. Obviously, it wasn't to find money in Jake's safe. No such money existed. No, they wanted her to insinuate herself into Jake's confidence, that was clear enough, and then … But she didn't know, couldn't know until she discovered more about Jake's enemies, for they were certainly that.

Jake. She pictured his face, flushed with exertion and happiness, as they moved into each other's arms in the gazebo. He was so extraordinarily handsome, with his forceful, angular face and dark, intense eyes, handsome, debonair, delightful, the man she'd always hoped to meet. Right now, at this moment, he cared for her. She knew it and she knew, too, that he had a rock hard streak in him, a dislike of sham and dishonesty, and what would happen if she had to tell him the truth of how they'd met and had to tell him she was an actress?

She remembered his face that first afternoon, the anger, and how she'd wanted, desperately, to have him smile at her. What kind of anger would transform his face if he learned that their encounter was planned, staged to the last detail? No matter how it hurt, no matter how clearly she saw the outcome, she knew as the plane bounced across the Monterey runway that she had to tell him – and tell him now. The implications were too serious, the possibilities too frightful to ignore. It was a set-up, of course, some kind of terribly complicated set-up. She couldn't guess the ultimate objective, but the sooner Jake knew the sooner he could fight back. He could contact the police, hire a private detective, do whatever was necessary to discover the reasons behind this charade.

If, along the way, he broke her heart, well, that was the price and she would pay it to protect him.

She carried that hard burden with her as she drove from the airport to her apartment. She climbed the steps slowly, unlocked the door, and stood wearily in the small living room. She'd left that morning full of hope, determined to convince the FBI its investigation was skewed. Now she faced the dreadful task of destroying a love that had just begun, a wonderful, fresh, happy love that lightened her heart and her life.

She had to tell him and she had to do it now.

Kirsten turned and walked across the braided, circular rug to the wooden counter that separated the living room from the kitchen. She reached out to pick up the telephone receiver, then her hand paused. The red message light glowed.

Only Jake Johnson, someone at the Johnson house or the pseudo Ellis Kemp knew she was in Carmel.

She took a deep breath and picked up the receiver. The night clerk came on the line and she asked for her message.

"Someone left a letter for you this afternoon. It's here at the desk."

Kirsten hurried downstairs. She took the envelope and returned to her apartment and ripped open the letter the minute she stepped inside. At first, she felt an overwhelming wave of relief and happiness when she saw the message was from Jake; then she realized the message complicated everything. She reread the message:

Dear Kirsten,

An urgent matter is recalling me to Washington. I'm enclosing a plane ticket for you. Will you please come? Call and let me know when to pick you up.

I'm already missing you.

Love,

Jake

Through her fatigue and worry, she smiled at his scrawling signature. It was as angular and abrupt as his face and as unmistakably his. Then her smile faded and she began to pace up and down. Jake wasn't here. He was in Washington so what should she do? It was Friday night. Even if she could reach him by telephone, this wasn't something that could be explained that way. Would only a few hours make a difference? Tomorrow, Saturday, she was supposed to meet her contact in San Francisco in the heart of Chinatown at Portsmouth Square.

Did she dare wait to tell Jake? She nodded her head decisively. It would only be a matter of a day at the most. She would go into San Francisco for the rendezvous tomorrow and fly to Washington that afternoon or Sunday. He'd asked her to call and let him know when she would arrive. Could she talk to him and not betray herself? Well, she was an actress. Had it ever been more important for her to act?

The call went through and Amy answered. Kirsten wondered if there were a hint of reserve, almost dislike, in Amy's voice before she put the call through to Jake, then Kirsten chided herself. She would be seeing conspirators in every shadow if she weren't careful. But a conspirator existed, must exist, on Jake's staff, so …

Then he was on the line and she forgot her fears and almost her worries at the sound of his voice.

"Kirsten, did you get my note?"

"Yes, and I'd love to come."

"Great." His voice boomed over the wire. "What time will you get in?"

"I'm not sure. I'll call back tomorrow. I have to meet with a director in San Francisco tomorrow morning, but I'll fly out that afternoon or Sunday,"

"I'll count the hours."

"I will, too."

After she hung up, she rested her hand for a long moment on the receiver, but the warmth and reassurance of his voice was gone and she was back with her fears.

She was supposed to make contact tomorrow at Portsmouth Square.

Her instructions were clear: Deliver a report on her search of the senator's study along with the key to the safe and the camera. She'd thought, of course, when she received the instructions and believed them to be coming from the FBI that the purpose was clear and aboveboard, provide a report on her actions and supply the evidence, via the photographs, plus return the key to the safe. Now she knew the report was a sham, but, of course, the return of the key and the camera were all important to her employers. Without them, she would have nothing tangible to prove her story that she'd been hired as part of a sting operation. The minute she gave up the camera and the key, all she had was her word – and who was going to believe it?

So she wasn't going to play their game. No indeed. She would hang onto the camera and the key. They might make all the difference one day when she talked to the real FBI. But she could do more than that. She could turn the tables – and she would – tomorrow, at Portsmouth Square.

The paunchy man wiped his face with the back of his hand. It was damn hot in the ill-smelling phone booth, but some calls he made only from public phones even though he knew his lines at the used car lot weren't tapped. He'd survived for a long, long time by being careful and he wasn't about to be careless now. Southern California had a barbaric climate for all the sentimentalizing about it. Give him a crisp fresh morning in the Dolomites any time. He grunted as he dialed the last digit.

A husky voice answered. "Billy,"

The paunchy man dealt with all kinds, some as close to pure evil as the world produced, but the sound of that husky voice chilled even him. He spoke briskly to ward off a shudder. "Michael here. That special assignment we spoke about. Today's the day. You have her picture…"

A sudden high giggle made him pause. "It's a pretty picture, but she won't be so pretty…"

Michael interrupted sharply. "Remember, it has to look like an accident. Do you understand? There can't be any suggestion of murder."

Billy's giggle died away to be replaced with a sullen silence and Michael could picture him on the other end of the line with his choirboy's face marred only by eyes that were never still but always moving restlessly.

"You understand?" Michael repeated.

Saturday morning, Kirsten called the Johnson house and talked to Jake's mother.

"I've lost a compact. I think it must have fallen out the day we took a drive in the Fiat. Would you mind if I ran by the house to check?"

Jake's mother welcomed her a few minutes later and even led the way to the garages.

"It's so quiet here when everyone's gone."

"Did Amy and Drew go back to Washington with Jake?"

"Oh, yes. He depends upon them so. I don't know what he'd do without them. And Murray, of course."

Kirsten chattered pleasantly but she was thinking of Jake's staff, placid-faced Amy and languid Drew and the somehow-frightening Murray. Was one of them involved in the conspiracy against Jake? The answer had to be yes. But which? His best friend's widow? His cousin? The man who saved his life in Vietnam? The old feeling of unreality swept over her. If she didn't know that something peculiar was happening, if she weren't living proof of it, she would feel that she'd imagined it all. Certainly if there were an undercurrent of hostility to Jake, surely his mother would have sensed it. There was nothing in Mrs. Johnson's demeanor to suggest anything other than the best of all possible worlds for her son.

Then Kirsten stared at the license plate on the back of the Fiat. Somehow, she forced herself to go through the motions of searching for the compact even as she struggled against the rush of disappointment. The numbers didn't jibe with those given to her by the L.A. building manager.

But all the way back up the graveled path toward the front of the rambling house and the turnaround drive, she was seeing the numbers of the Fiat license plate – and they weren't the numbers given to her by the building manager in L.A. She'd been so certain, so sure that she finally had one tiny piece of concrete evidence, and now once again she had nothing – nothing but her own suspicions, her own certainty that whatever threatened Jake Johnson had its origins close to him. How else explain that incredibly intimate portrait in the materials the "agent" had given her to study? How else had the "agent" known that Jake would be in Carmel? Everyone in his Washington office thought he was in New York. Only Amy and Drew and Murray, and, of course, his mother, knew he would take those stolen days in Carmel. That drew a tight, close circle, didn't it?

She thanked Mrs. Johnson again and guided the dark red Porsche out of the drive and turned toward the Carmel gate. She would take the inland route to

San Francisco, of course, to make better speed. Once past the gate, she turned left onto State Highway No.1.

She never even saw the double-tired, low-slung black Ford pickup that growled to life and fell in behind her.

Billy didn't mind the three-hour drive to San Francisco. He liked to drive. He liked to drive and play games in his mind with the people he saw, what he could do to them if he wished and how they had no idea of it. That amused him. It was too bad about the girl. He could really have enjoyed himself with her. Girls were always fun because at first they didn't believe him. They looked at his face, and he knew how handsome he was and how much he looked like everybody's kid brother, and that made it so much more fun when they finally realized and became afraid. That was the part he enjoyed the most, watching the slow dawning of fear and horror, all because of him, when he willed it. But not this time. This time it had to look like an accident. It wouldn't be hard. When she started back to Carmel, he would pick his time. His pickup could maneuver her Porsche off the road anytime he wanted to; and, if he sideswiped her along the coast where the road ran along the cliffs, it would be as neat an accident as anybody ever engineered.

Jake Johnson hurried down the Capitol steps, frowning. The situation certainly warranted a special meeting of the Senate Select Committee on Intelligence. Matters were coming to a head in El Salvador and, as always, the options were few and the problems intransigent. He felt the old flame of anger. Why was the United States so often in the posture of supporting a repressive regime against the legitimate aspirations of the people, and when would they stop equating every nationalist movement with the evils of Communism? It was time the Americans worked to support American ideals, liberty for all. It was time American politicians had the courage to stand up against armed American intervention to bolster regimes that maintained power through death squads and intimidation. As he strode toward his car, he was still frowning. It would take courage, political courage, because the opposition would try to label them isolationists, or, worse, soft on communism. He'd talk it over with Kirsten. His quick stride slowed and he began to smile. Last week, he would have talked it over with Drew or Amy. Now, his first thought was Kirsten. She would arrive either this evening or tomorrow. He could tell her of the bad news the Committee had received and how he'd responded. Yes, he would tell her that and he would listen to her response and then he would make love to her and her thoughts and her being were equally important to him. Kirsten. She was so lovely and lively and, suddenly, he felt so young again. He began to whistle and, once more, his stride lengthened despite the sultry haze of August in Washington, D.C.

Kirsten stopped in Monterey and made her purchases. She carried them in a raffia basket that she plumped into the passenger seat of the Porsche. She didn't notice the black Ford pickup that left the shopping center behind her. Back on the highway, she drove automatically, thinking over her plan. She didn't see any loopholes, and, once the afternoon was over, she should be in a much stronger position – if all went as she hoped.

She drove too fast, chafing at the traffic though she knew she couldn't expect it any other way, because this was the height of the tourist season. Then the city rose on its hills ahead of her and the old magic caught at her heart. It didn't matter how many times she saw the lovely city by the bay, each time was as exciting and promising as the first. Someday she and Jake would come together and he could wear his levis and dark glasses and a painter's cap and they would wander hand in hand up and down the steep, hilly streets and stop to laugh at the mimes and to clap for the street dancers and to feel sorry for the leashed monkey performing to the high strains of an accordion. They would eat chocolate at Ghirardelli Square and fresh abalone at Fisherman's Wharf. They would laugh and enjoy each other and the lovely city by the bay.

But not today.

Kirsten turned up Columbus and took it all the way to Washington and turned left. The Holiday Inn loomed ahead, and directly across the street lay Portsmouth Square. She turned into the hotel parking garage. She carried the raffia basket with her as she took the elevator up to the lobby.

A black Ford pickup waited its turn behind the Porsche to be parked.

10

KIRSTEN DUMPED OUT THE contents of the raffia basket on the double bed. She picked up the wig first and turned to the mirror along the wall. The wig fit sleekly, the thick black hair twisted back into a chignon. The difference in her appearance was startling. Her fair skin seemed almost luminescent framed by the vividly black hair. She took out her pencil lipstick and leaned close to the mirror. She worked slowly and carefully, exaggerating the shape of her mouth with darkly red lipstick, utterly different from her usual pale pink. She took her newly purchased blush, a bright and deep red, and arched spots of color on her cheeks. Then she put on the silver-mirrored sunglasses and surveyed her face. It was perfect. No one would see through this disguise. She wasn't quite finished. She slipped out of her pale blue blouse and white slacks and pulled on the shapeless dark brown Mexican dress she'd also bought in Monterey. Then, with a final satisfied look in the mirror, she turned to go.

Portsmouth Square was on two levels, but what in San Francisco wasn't? Kirsten walked slowly, aimlessly, pausing often to admire the well-kept beds of flowers. She bought a Coke at a stand. She spotted her contact on her first round of the park but passed her by with only a glance. Kirsten felt a little surprised when she realized her contact was the same woman she'd met at the Huntington Galleries. This time the woman wore a shabby magenta sweater and a heavy, tweedy gray skirt. The woman sat alone on a concrete bench, reading a copy of *Time*. Most of the people in the park were elderly Chinese, sitting quietly on the benches in the pale afternoon sunlight. Some of the men played chess. The old ladies, dressed in shapeless black slacks, talked amiably, their string bags carefully positioned between them on the benches.

Kirsten settled on a bench slightly behind her quarry and unfolded a copy of the *Examiner*.

Her contact began to check her watch every few minutes as the time for their meeting came and passed. The woman waited for a full hour beyond the scheduled time, then slowly, heavily, rose and walked north.

Kirsten folded her paper and started after her. When they reached Columbus, the woman stopped at a bus stop. Kirsten turned and looked in a shop window and realized this was an adult bookstore and moved to the next shop, an Italian bakery. Two busses came and went. The woman boarded the third, No. 41, and Kirsten ran up the steps at the last minute. She walked to the back of the bus and sat where she could keep a close watch on her quarry.

The bus rumbled out Columbus then turned west on Union. Kirsten watched the neighborhood with interest as they passed light blue and yellow and pink Victorian homes with bay windows and dormers. Obviously, the woman was going home. Once Kirsten knew where she lived, well, that would be the first step in finding out who was behind the conspiracy. The woman had no idea she was being followed, that was obvious. She slumped in her bus seat, her head turned toward the window. Soon, in only a few more minutes, Kirsten was going to be one up on her adversaries. It would be like picking up a tangle of cord. Once she found a free end and gave a yank, the whole mess would straighten out. It might be too early to scent victory, but she couldn't help feeling superior. So they, whoever they were, thought Kirsten Soderstrom was a fool and a dupe. Well, they were going to have a surprise coming to them, and she was just the woman to administer it. With pleasure.

The minute her quarry began to stir, Kirsten tensed. Yes, the woman was yanking the cord and standing. Kirsten waited until the last minute, then moved after her. When they stood on the sidewalk, Kirsten paused as if looking at directions. The woman started up a steep hill.

Kirsten glanced at the street sign. Baker Street. She almost smiled because she certainly did feel like a Baker Street Irregular and that was a nice coincidence. She was still smiling as she started up the hill. She wondered which of the Victorian homes was the woman's objective. Kirsten would get the address then check a phone book, find out the name of the resident. She was going to have some information in hand when she talked to Jake.

For an instant, her excitement and feeling of accomplishment wavered. Their love was so new, so tenuous, and it had the quality of the newborn, needing nurture and care and gentleness, unable to survive harshness and ill treatment. He would be angry, so angry, when he discovered that their meeting was prearranged because he couldn't help but wonder whether all of her behavior was designed to entrap him. Oh, surely she could convince him, but her sense of coldness and dismay persisted.

She picked up her pace. The woman was at the end of the block. She'd passed by all the lovely homes. She was crossing the street. Kirsten could see the sign now. Green Street. The woman turned right and walked along the chest-high iron fence; then she paused, opened a gate, and walked up to the building that sat on the northeast corner. Kirsten frowned. That wasn't a home. It was too big. Maybe she worked there … but it didn't look commercial. The building was six stories tall with a partial seventh floor. The first story was faced with gray stone in horizontal stripes. The windows on the ground floor were barred. The upper stories were of a tan yellow brick.

Kirsten crossed Green and turned right and then she stood in front of the main gate, locked now. Inside the gate, three steps led up to a brown wooden double door beneath an archway.

From where she stood, she could the broad sweep of San Francisco Bay sparkling in the August sunlight. She could also see the brass plate on the left hand side of the door of the building at 2790 Green Street.

The brass plate contained the legend: Consulate of the Union of Soviet Socialist Republics.

Numbly, Kirsten turned and retraced her steps, walking down Baker Street.

Consulate of the Union of Soviet Socialist Republics. The Russians. The Communists.

What had she become involved in? She had never given much thought to the stiff relations between America and Russia, but she hadn't been surprised by the Russian boycott of the Olympics in Los Angeles, either.

Somehow, she managed to keep walking. She even hailed a cab and gave the address of the Holiday Inn on Kearney in an even voice and sat in the back of the cab, her face expressionless, but panic flooded her mind.

Once back in the hotel room she sank into a chair by the balcony window and faced the truth.

She was involved, seriously, devastatingly, with an enemy agent. The man who'd called himself Ellis Kemp was a Russian agent. That was clear enough now. What wasn't clear was the motive.

He'd hired her to get to know Jake Johnson on the pretext that Johnson was taking bribes and she would discover the evidence for the FBI.

That was all a lie.

But she'd been hired for a purpose.

Not, obviously, to find evidence against Jake Johnson. That hadn't been the purpose at all. Still, they'd gone to a lot of trouble to get a key to Jake's study safe. Why did they want her to open the safe? That was all she'd done, open the safe and move and photograph its contents …

Her heart began to thud. The safe and its contents – she closed her eyes, squeezed them shut in concentration. Those folders – there were two both of them, blue-backed and both stamped SECRET – CONFIDENTIAL.

Kirsten opened her eyes and stared stonily out the window. That was it, of course. The information in those folders must be important to the Russians and she was the decoy. She would be willing to bet her life that the contents of those folders were even now being studied at a desk of the KGB off Red Square. Someone had copied those files and provided them to the Russians, someone on Jake's staff, and she was hired to be the false trail for the CIA when the information surfaced in Russia. Who would ever believe her wild story of FBI agents and casting offices and undercover sting operations? She had no proof. All she had was meetings with a Russian national that she could never explain satisfactorily. If the U.S. government complained about the activity of the woman from the Russian Consulate, the Russians would send her back to Moscow and Kirsten could protest until hell froze over that she'd thought the woman an FBI contact and no one would believe her.

Kirsten wearily got up from the chair and walked into the bathroom. She scrubbed the makeup from her face and pulled off the wig and brushed her hair. When she was dressed in her own clothes, she bundled up the wig and Mexican dress and stuffed them in the raffia basket.

All right. She was still a tiny step ahead of the Russians. At least, she didn't have to call her adversaries 'they' anymore. Now, she knew who they were. They still thought she was the gull. While they felt secure, she would reach Jake and tell him everything and they would call in the CIA and, whether anyone believed her or not she would get them started investigating, and maybe somewhere along the way something would surface to support her story.

Jake would believe her. Her heart twisted inside. Please, let Jake believe her.

She checked out and hurried down to the parking garage. She tossed the basket into the back seat and turned right on Kearney. She paid no attention to the car behind her.

Billy was smiling as he turned the double-tired black Ford pickup to the right on Kearney. Excitement bubbled deep inside him.

Michael reached for the glass of iced tea. He drank thirstily. Patches of sweat made enormous crescents under the arms of his shirt. The rattle of traffic from La Brea made it seem even hotter in the stuffy used-car office, and the window air-conditioner pulled in the sooty smog-laden air. The phone would ring soon and that would mark the end of it – and the end of that pretty little blonde. The Senator had turned out to like blondes, that was right enough. It was too bad she'd had to go, but necessary, very necessary. He squinted in thought and retraced the plan in his mind. Her fingerprints were in the safe. Today, when she made contact with Iva, she was to hand in her report, the key and the camera. They would plant the key and camera in her Carmel apartment to be found by the CIA. The meeting today was crucial. Kurt was stationed nearby, poised to photograph Kirsten handing the material to Iva. That was the linchpin of the entire plan, the ultimate proof that she was a traitor. They would have to sacrifice Iva, of course, but that was a small matter. The U.S. could do nothing more than demand her recall. Iva'd wanted to go home for several years. It would all work out. The photograph would be indisputable evidence – and Kirsten wouldn't be able to deny it. She would be dead. Once again, he felt a small stirring of regret. She was a lovely thing, like a wildflower in the early morning, a hint of freshness. Too bad. Too bad. Then he shook the thought away. He'd planned it down to the last detail. The photograph of Kirsten and Iva meeting would be received by the CIA, anonymously, of course, in the mail next Wednesday. The Amraam plans would be in Moscow by then and, of course, the CIA would know. They always knew. He turned his mind to the imposing KGB headquarters off Red Square. Who was the CIA mole? Was it someone he knew? The mole had escaped detection for many years now, but he was quick and accurate. Their own man at Langley would report when the CIA heard of the loss of the plans. Then the CIA would swing into high gear and the queries would go out and it would be only a matter of hours, perhaps even minutes, before the CIA realized that one Senator Jacob Holland Johnson had the Amraam plans in his possession during the critical hours.

Michael's mouth spread in a broad, satisfied smile. From there, it would be child's play, and he was the one who had set it up. It would probably ruin the senator's career. He might even be suspected of collusion. That would be a plus. He'd been a thorn in their side for years now. Johnson's staff member who passed the information for one hundred thousand dollars in cash would be safely hidden behind Kirsten – and that was good because close scrutiny might lead to Michael. Michael frowned. He'd not liked the fact that he'd met with the staffer several times. That was the only weak link in the plan, but so long as Kirsten was suspected …

The phone rang.

He finished the glass of tea and looked in surprise at the wall clock. It was a little early for Billy to call. He began to frown. If that vicious little killer had screwed up … He yanked the receiver off the cradle.

He made Iva repeat it twice. Then he sat there, his heavy face curdled with anger. The little blonde bitch. She hadn't shown up. She hadn't shown up! They didn't have the photograph of her passing material to Iva. For Christ's sake, they didn't have anything. And right now, his stomach churned, right now, the blond killer was following her, waiting for the right moment.

Kirsten decided against taking 101 south. The traffic would be heavy and she felt, despite the curves, she could make almost as good time on the coast road and she needed time to think. She'd left the key to Jake's safe and the camera shaped like a compact in her Carmel apartment. She would pick them up, then fly from Monterey to San Francisco and from there to Washington. The road began to curl and curve around the coastline and the cliffs fell away to her right. She looked at the spectacular scenery, the bright black of the basalt rocks. Fine curtains of spume glittered like winter frost. She wished Jake were there to share the loveliness with her. Jake. Would he understand? Would he believe her? She wanted to go even faster, but she knew she couldn't, not and make the plunging curves with any margin of safety. She pushed the Porsche as fast as she dared on the curving road. She loved the feel of power beneath her hands, the sense of mastery in controlling the fine car. It would be fun to race this car. For just an instant she was carried back across the years to the thrill and danger of dirt bikes and her father's pride when she won. She was good at machines. She always had been.

She glanced in her rearview mirror. A black Ford pickup hung close behind her. She frowned. He was a little too close. She didn't like tailgaters. There wasn't much traffic. She picked up her speed a little. The Ford picked up speed, too.

The Porsche reached a crest and began a sharp hairpin curve. For an instant, Kirsten forgot the irritation of the truck behind her because the view was so magnificent. There was only a narrow roadside barrier between her and the edge of the cliff.

It was the sound that warned her, the unmistakable roar of a gunning motor.

Her head jerked up and she looked in her rearview mirror. At first, she didn't understand. Was he out of his mind? Did he want to kill all of them?

She saw his face in her side mirror, a broad, young face with wide-spaced, angelic blue eyes and curly blond hair. He was smiling and, as he pulled out beside her and began to pressure her car toward the railing and the plummeting fall to the ocean rocks, his smile widened.

Then she had no time for thought or fear or even for the hot surge of anger that flickered deep inside. She had thought only for the hurtling piece of steel that she rode and would ride to her death if the black pickup caromed against the Porsche and pushed it through the railing.

She remembered then how it was, how you had to keep your nerve and not give into pressure even though it seemed the next instant you would lock wheels and crash into a heap. She watched out of the corner of her eye while she held the Porsche steady, then, at the last moment, anticipating the sideways movement of the pickup, she jammed on her brakes. The pickup roared past and she glimpsed his face again and he wasn't smiling now. Anger twisted those angelic features, anger and something more, something infinitely ugly.

Kirsten clung to the steering wheel and kept the Porsche on the road and now she was behind the pickup.

It had taken only seconds, the stretch of road empty except for the two of them, the heart stopping moment when the pickup roared to the left of her, pushing her toward death. Then the moment was past and the truck was past. They came around the curve. There was traffic in front of them and a battered station wagon coming up behind them, but Kirsten knew near-death had happened and knew that her peril continued. It wasn't chance or a random attack. The moment was too well chosen for that. She clung to the steering wheel and watched the pickup in front of her and realized coldly and calmly that she had played out her usefulness for the Russians and now it was time to make it impossible for her to proclaim her innocence. It was all very simple. The scenario was written. Exit, Kirsten. But she didn't like her role, thank you very much, and she wasn't playing any longer.

Unfortunately, no one had told the driver of the pickup that the play was over and she was stuck on a two-lane road behind him. She reached over and opened the glove compartment and poked around and found a crumpled map. She spread it open and took quick glances. Yes, there was a turn-off in about six miles. She swallowed. He would come after her, of course, and the road would be a narrow, twisting one across the rugged hills, but it was her only chance.

He slowed down as they neared the intersection but she didn't brake until the last minute, then she jammed the brakes, wrenched the wheel to the right and sped off, the speedometer climbing, forty, fifty, sixty, seventy miles an hour on the narrow mountainous road. She squealed around curves, plunged down steep valleys, and tore up the other side. She watched the rearview. If he caught up with her now … Then she saw another road. She braked again, swung the car to the right, and felt a glow of triumph. He hadn't been behind her. He couldn't possibly know she'd taken this back road. Quickly, she backed and turned the Porsche the way she'd come. Then she parked well in the shadow of a fir tree and opened the door and ran back to the road. Taking cover behind another fir, she waited. The black pickup roared past. He didn't spare a glance for the side road.

Kirsten turned the Porsche back to the coast road. She drove very fast now, with a wary eye for any cars that seemed to linger near. As soon as possible, she cut through the hills to 101 and drove as fast as she dared. This wouldn't be the day to pick up a ticket. How long would it take the driver of the black Ford pickup to report his failure? Of course, he could have reached a phone by now. Would they be waiting for her at the apartment in Carmel?

She looked at it from every angle, but she needed the camera and the key

That's all she had by way of proof. They wouldn't expect her to come to the apartment. They would believe she was fully forewarned.

Did she dare try to reach the apartment?

11

JAKE JOHNSON SAT IN his study and stared at the report spread out in front of him. Drew had done an excellent job, putting together a cogent analysis of voting trends in California in the recent state elections. This kind of information could make or break his race next year, but he hadn't even flipped to the second page. Instead, he looked at the clock: nine o'clock. It would be six o'clock in California and why hadn't Kirsten called?

What if she never called, never came?

She should have called by now if she were coming. He frowned. She was going into San Francisco to meet with a producer. Wasn't that what she'd said? Well, it couldn't take all day. She should have called and said she was arriving tonight or in the morning. Why hadn't she called?

Abruptly, he pushed the buzzer on his desk, held. In a moment, Amy opened the door and looked at him inquiringly.

"Amy." He heard the sharp note in his voice and saw her look at him in surprise. "Sorry.

He tried to sound pleasant. "I didn't mean to snap at you, but are you sure Kirsten didn't call today?"

"Absolutely certain," she responded coldly. "I make a record of all incoming calls."

"Right." He looked at the telephone.

She waited for a moment in the doorway. "Will there be anything else?"

"No. Not tonight."

When the door closed behind her, he grimaced. He was making a damn fool of himself. Amy must think he'd lost his mind to question her about calls. Of course, she would have told him if Kirsten had called. He might as well face it. She wasn't going to call. For an instant, he was swept by the deepest wave of depression and feeling of loss. For God's sake, maybe he was losing his grip. She was just a girl, just another beautiful girl.

But that wasn't true, that would never be true.

All day he'd looked forward to her call. He'd planned everything they would do and see. He would show her the Washington he loved, the city of parks and avenues with the grand vista down Pennsylvania Avenue and the spectacular view of the Capitol. He would take her first to Mt. Vernon. He loved going there, loved the sense of history, the beauty of the mansion overlooking the Potomac, the musty smell of dust and age and the delight of picturing in his mind the clever and disciplined man who'd led a ragtag band of revolutionaries to success. He had planned their first day – and night – and now there was only silence.

Kirsten – he remembered the last time they'd made love and the softness in her eyes. He knew the way her silver blonde hair swept back from her forehead and how her laughter sounded, light and clear like bells in a Swiss village, and the grace of her walk. He knew these things and knew that she excited and pleased him as no other woman, even Francesca, ever had.

Why didn't she call?

She'd dropped into his life one sunny afternoon and he'd felt young again, alive, eager. Now there was only silence.

Why didn't she call?

A pulse throbbed in Amy's throat. She walked down the hall and heard her heels clicking against the hardwood floor. She knew she sounded angry. Well, she was angry. She turned into the drawing room and, for once, the enormous high ceilings and the muted grays and blues of the old Persian rug didn't charm her. She dropped into a chintz-covered chair in front of the sofa and snatched up her magazine.

Drew's head jerked up. "For God's sake, Amy, do you have to stalk down the hall?"

She glared at him. "You're as jumpy as a cat tonight, Drew. What's your problem?"

Drew blew out his breath in an irritated spurt. "Same thing's bothering everybody else. He's in a really lousy mood, isn't he?"

"You're right on target," she said sardonically.

Drew stared at her. "You didn't get a call from her?"

Amy slammed down her magazine. "For God's sake, would I keep it a secret?"

He held up his hands in apology. "Sorry. But it makes you wonder, doesn't it?"

Amy stared at him for a long moment. "No," she said finally. "It doesn't make me wonder at all. Frankly, I don't give a damn."

Michael rolled the cold cigar in his fingers, around and around and around. Why hadn't the girl shown up at Portsmouth Square? Everything hinged on the reason why. She wasn't back in her apartment, at least not yet. Thank God Billy hadn't succeeded in pushing her off the road. Marko was watching the apartment with instructions to call him immediately if she arrived. She would arrive if her reason for missing the contact were innocent. She wouldn't if she suspected the truth. Would she decide the episode with Billy was random, the kind of mad and terrible thing that happened in an area teeming with millions, or would she link in her mind the black truck with Carmel and the senator? It could go either way. So now, he had to wait. If she didn't come, then he'd have to get the word out, start the search for her. It was essential that she be seen making contact with a Russian agent. Otherwise, the link wouldn't be there when the CIA realized the Amraam papers were in Moscow. Of course, if she'd tumbled to the program he would have to do it another way. There were always other ways.

It was dark by the time she reached Carmel. Kirsten parked on Dolores Street near Fourth. She'd made two stops in Monterey, one at a five-and-dime where she bought a whistle and the second at a beachfront shop where she bought a pair of used Levis and a jeans jacket and a soft cap. She stuffed her hair up under the cap and changed to the jeans and jacket in a gas station restroom. In the dark, she could easily pass for a teenage boy.

She didn't go to the front entrance of the apartment unit. Instead, she walked quickly up a back alley, past mimosa trees and hibiscus and a thick patch of monkey grass. The motel apartments were in a three-story wooden building with outside entrances. Kirsten stood beneath a weeping willow and watched her door. There was no light on in the apartment. She waited while two couples came down the stairs, chatting good humoredly. There was nothing out of the way, nothing off key.

When she walked up the steps, she passed her door once and went to the next apartment. It too was unlit. She knocked, but no one came. Finally, she turned and retraced her steps, then, swiftly, she unlocked her door and slipped inside and turned on the light. She faced the apartment living area and in her hand she held the whistle, ready to blow if anyone were there. The apartment appeared undisturbed. Kirsten moved quickly. She hurried to the bedroom and lifted up the corner of the bed and slipped out the camera and the key and dropped them into her pocket.

Although nothing had happened to indicate anyone was near at all, she felt uneasy and in a hurry to be gone. She certainly didn't want to come face to face with that murderous blond or with the heavy featured man who ...

The ring of the telephone exploded in the quiet of the bedroom.

Kirsten whirled around and faced the phone and looked at it as she might a snake.

It rang once, twice, a third time.

Slowly, Kirsten reached out and picked up the receiver.

"Hello."

There was a long pause. She could hear a man's heavy breathing. Then he spoke. "Miss Soderstrom?"

She recognized his voice, of course, recognized it and wondered wildly why he called, but if he were on the phone he couldn't be walking in the door, unless he were calling to catch her and the blond killer was on his way. Should she talk or should she run?

"Miss Soderstrom?" His voice was sharp now.

"Yes." She paused, then asked smoothly, "Who is this, please?" and all the while she watched the door and held the whistle.

"This is Ellis Kemp."

Kirsten felt a shock of triumph. He was calling himself Ellis Kemp. By God, he didn't know that she'd found him out. He thought she still believed him to be an FBI agent. Oh, she needed to step carefully here, step very carefully indeed, but this was her chance to set up some kind of contact with him.

"Oh, Mr. Kemp," she said and relief sounded in her voice, throbbed in her voice. "I'm so glad you called. The worst thing happened today at Portsmouth Square. Someone was following me, I'm just sure of it."

He didn't say a word. She could imagine him thinking, trying to figure out what it could mean.

"Followed you? What makes you think so?"

"I'm positive. I went to the Holiday Inn across the street from the Square." He would know that, of course, because the blond young man in the black pickup must have followed her there so she must stick as close to the truth as possible. "I parked and then I went across to the Square and just before I was going to sit down by the woman, you know, she was carrying a purple purse just as my instructions said, well, just before I was going to sit down with her, I saw this man looking at me." Her voice rose. "It shocked me, I can tell you."

"What did he do?"

"He looked at me." Kirsten said it in a hushed tone. "I knew at once that I had to be careful. I mean, what if the people who are paying off the Senator have heard some rumor of a sting? That could be. I knew I'd better not make contact, so I just hurried right on out of the park and took a bus up Columbus and got off and walked around then I caught a taxi back to the hotel and drove to Carmel, and that was awful, too. I couldn't believe it but this kid tried to run me off the road."

She could imagine the thoughts running though his mind: was she really quite as stupid as she sounded, could she possible have misinterpreted some man's passing interest in a solitary woman as a kind of surveillance and fled the park?

She didn't want him to ponder too long. She gave a huge sigh. "I'm so tired but now I have to hurry and pack and ..."

"Pack? Your instructions are to meet your contact and turn in the materials that ..."

"It will have to be in Washington," she said briskly. "I'm just on my way out the door. You can call me at the Senator's and ..."

"Miss Soderstrom, your duties are finished. All that remains …"

"Oh no," she retorted. "Once I start a job, I finish it, and I want you to know, Mr. Kemp, I think I'm on to something bigger than you imagined. I'm pretty certain the Senator isn't being paid off by anybody and I think someone on his staff … Oh, I've got to go. My plane leaves in just a few minutes. Call me in Virginia."

She slammed down the phone and regarded it with a good deal of amusement when it began to ring. She ignored it and swiftly dumped some clothes into a suitcase, grabbed up her purse, and hurried out the door. The phone was still ringing. Kirsten grinned as she ran down the steps. That may not have been a smart move, but she'd bet she had Mr. Kemp's attention and she'd bet, too, that he would indeed get in touch with her in Virginia and that should please the CIA.

She went out the back way again, but she'd only gone a half block when she realized she was being followed, and a very cold feeling made her chest ache. But, if harm were intended, why hadn't the man pushed his way into her apartment? She didn't know, but she knew that her opponents were capable of anything. That had been proved by the young man in the black pickup. She didn't intend to be stopped, not now, not after all she'd been through. She had a deep-seated feeling, almost a sense of compulsion, that she must reach Jake, that she must tell him face to face what had happened. Nothing else would suffice and nobody was going to stop her now.

She began to walk quickly. The man behind her picked up his pace. As she turned the corner, she glanced back as he passed under the street lamp, short, stocky, sandy haired with glasses, wearing brown slacks and a tan polo shirt, designed to disappear in a crowd. Okay, fella …

She turned into a bar and had the hostess seat her, gave her order then slipped out of the seat and turned down a corridor toward the restrooms. She smiled to herself as she stepped into the kitchen. She handed a startled bus boy ten dollars. "This will cover my drink and give you some left over if you can show me the back door."

He looked at her blankly.

"There's a man I want to avoid."

"Oh. Okay. Right this way."

Out in the alley, she didn't waste time. She ran lightly, her eyes adjusting to the dark. She stayed in the alley for two blocks, then cut back to her left and found the Porsche. No one was behind her.

It was a long drive down the coast but she was sure "Mr. Kemp" would expect her to fly out of San Francisco and she intended to make a career, though she hoped a brief one, of disappointing "Mr. Kemp."

Dawn was breaking when she reached the airport. Even the L.A. International Airport slumbered at five on Sunday morning. Kirsten kept a close watch on the occasional passersby but no one paid the slightest attention to her. When she exchanged the ticket Jake had given her for a seat on an American flight into National that would take off in half an hour, she began to feel the tickle of success. Then the feeling of elation subsided. She had to call Jake.

What was she going to tell him?

Jake was drinking a second cup of coffee on the terrace when Amy came to the French windows.

"It's Kirsten, Jake. Long distance."

He reached his desk in the study in record time.

"Kirsten?" He could feel his heart beating and he was absurdly excited and happy.

"Jake, I just have a minute. I'm at the Los Angeles airport …" She talked fast. "Lots has happened since yesterday and I'll tell you all about it when I get in." She gave him the flight number and arrival time. Then she paused, "Jake, oh Jake, I love you so much."

Jake heard the words, words which should delight him, but there was something in her tone, something driven and half frightened …

"Kirsten, what's wrong?"

He heard a ragged half-breath on the other end then she said quickly, unconvincingly, "I'm all right. Everything will be all right when I see you. Jake, do come, please. Be there."

"Of course, I'll be there. Kirsten, tell me, what's happened?"

Again, she said, "I love you," and the connection went dead.

Jake Johnson slowly hung up the telephone. What the hell? He shoved back his chair and walked across the room and out the French windows onto the terrace. All day yesterday he'd been uneasy, and now he felt certain there was a basis for his uneasiness. Something had disturbed Kirsten, disturbed her profoundly.

Jake jammed his hands in his trouser pockets and walked slowly down the terrace steps and out into the rose garden. A graveled path curved through the rose beds. The early morning dew still glistened on the creamy yellow and vivid crimson roses.

He loved this walk, through the banks of rose bushes, past the dogwood that turned spring into a lacy wonderland. He'd looked forward to showing all of this to Kirsten. He knew she would love it, would share with him the pleasure in the serene countryside.

What had happened to give her voice that tone of desperation, to make her say, as if uncertain of his response, that she loved him, and she wanted him to meet her?

He reached the edge of the pond. The ducks saw him and waddled out of the water, quacking beasts. They wanted a breakfast treat and he didn't have a scrap with him. He walked out onto a wooden bridge that spanned the softly-green water. Usually he loved coming here. After a difficult day on the Hill, he would hurry home and take the path to the pond and find peace in the gentle movement of the water. The graceful weeping willows on the shore swayed with the light breeze, reminding him of centuries-past cotillions and dancers long since turned to dust.

He found no peace this August morning. He gripped the railing and stared down into the water. A sudden harsh shower the night before had muddied the water. Usually, he could look deep into its clear green depths.

Kirsten's phone call, the call he'd so hoped for, that he'd feared would never come, worried him deeply. Her voice reflected the tension of someone laboring under great emotion. What could have happened, and why did it prompt her to say, desperately, that she loved him?

A small, cold center of fear flared deep inside.

Upstairs, a hand still rested on the telephone that had been softly and carefully replaced at the conclusion of Jake's conversation with Kirsten.

The blonde bitch was on her way! That didn't make sense. Something must have gone wrong in San Francisco because it was clearly understood, wasn't it. That the girl wouldn't return after she made contact at Portsmouth Square. That was the understanding. It would be disastrous if she were available for the CIA to interview when it became known that the Amraam papers had reached Moscow. She was to have disappeared and that would clinch it in the view of the CIA that she was the culprit, the only possible culprit.

For God's sake, something would have to be done.

12

KIRSTEN SAGGED BACK IN her seat. She'd not intended to break down like that on the phone. All she'd done now was to worry Jake. That would make their meeting even harder.

Jake – she remembered the first time she'd seen him, standing on the deck of his cruiser, and how magnificent he looked in a racing suit. She remembered how, finally, his generous mouth spread in a wonderful smile. She remembered the light of passion in his dark eyes and the feel of his body against hers and the incredible joy she'd shared with him. Would that mean enough to him to bridge the chasm she would open with her confession? Would he, could he understand and forgive?

"Another cup of coffee, Miss?"

Kirsten looked slowly up at the stewardess, a pretty girl with red hair, freckles, and a pleasant smile. Kirsten wondered what she would think if she knew what was in Kirsten's mind, but she only nodded yes and took the coffee and welcomed its heat through the thin plastic cup.

"Thank God for coffee, right?" The man sitting next to her was attractive, his dark hair frosted with gray. He had a genial smile and his eyes were looking at Kirsten with a great deal of interest.

She didn't want a plane conversation, not this morning, not with the burden of her thoughts and fears. She nodded politely and turned toward the window.

He wasn't to be discouraged quite so easily.

"Are you going to Washington for business or pleasure?

Kirsten said slowly, "I don't know. I wish I knew." She then looked again out the window and felt his shrug beside her. She drank the coffee and tried to imagine Jake's face when she told him.

Despite the coffee, she slept most of the way, awaking as the plane began its descent into National. She struggled awake and looked out the window, glimpsing the Capitol, glistening white in the bright morning sunlight, and the White House, unmistakable even from above. Quickly, combed her hair and wished she could do something about the shadows beneath her eyes. She glanced down at her green silk dress. It traveled well and looked much better than she felt. She'd changed from the Levis and jean jacket at the airport.

Actually, she looked fine, and that surprised her. The turmoil in her mind didn't show in her face or dress. She looked cool and self-possessed, but her hand opened and closed spasmodically on her purse. She carried the key to Jake's safe and the compact camera in the purse. The nearer the plane came to the runway, the more she dreaded what must happen.

Jake watched the jet throttle back, watched the nose dip down. Here it came. Easy does it. He didn't relax until the plane bumped once hard then settled onto the runway. He always dreaded landings at National with the short runways that gave no margin for error, but it was all right, it was fine, and Kirsten would be coming off the plane in only minutes. Then maybe the hard knot of anxiety in his stomach would dissolve.

He saw her, of course, the instant she was visible in the stream of passengers spilling into the reception area. She paused for an instant, framed in the exit way, and he marveled anew at her beauty. Heads turned to look at her. He felt a mixture of pride and jealousy and that surprised him because, really, he had no right to feel either. But it was thrilling to know that this spectacularly lovely woman raised her hand to him, moved toward him, moved eagerly, held out her arms to him.

He had always, even as a child, been loath to make public displays of affection. It wasn't in his nature. He was too controlled, his emotions always held in check by his mind. Yet, now, he felt himself move forward, taking great strides, and then he was taking Kirsten in his arms, picking her up, sweeping her around, then holding her tightly, pressing his face into the soft sweetness of her hair and murmuring her name, over and over.

They clung to each other then he heard the familiar crisp snap of a photographer's flash and he lifted his head.

"Hey, Senator, look this way, please, you and your friend."

Kirsten slipped out of his arms and turned her back to the camera, looking up at him for instruction.

He grinned down at her, appreciating her delicacy. It was a nice contrast to Francesca's inevitable grandstanding whenever the media appeared. Gently, he turned her back to face the camera along with him.

"One of my constituents," he called out to the photographer, and then he took Kirsten's hand and they walked down the concourse.

The photographer loped alongside them for a moment, asking for Kirsten's name.

At Jake's nod, Kirsten spelled it then said, "Huntington Beach," when asked for an address.

As they left the photographer behind, Jake looked at her ruefully. "I'm afraid that will make all the morning papers. Do you mind?"

"No." She paused, then said very low, "I hope that you won't mind."

So there it was again, the suggestion, no, more than that, the strong implication that there was something difficult to see faced.

He stopped and frowned and stared down into her face and he could see strain and worry and a kind of anguish that frightened him.

"Kirsten, what's wrong: You've got to tell me."

She nodded and swallowed hard then looked warily around at the travelers surging past them. "Let's wait until we're in the car, Jake."

So her arrival wasn't at all what he'd looked forward to. There was tension in the set of her shoulders and a lost and vulnerable look in the eyes that watched him as he drove toward the expressway.

When she did speak, her voice was low and weary.

"I have to tell you something very devastating, Jake. I hope you will let me tell it in my own way and that you will forgive me."

He didn't take his eyes from the road. "Are you still married?"

She looked surprised, then shook her head.

He felt a surge of relief and glanced at her and said, "Well, then, it can't be anything very bad." But she didn't smile in return.

Instead, she bit her lip then burst out, "My God, I don't know how to start so I guess I'll just blurt it out – Jake, someone on your staff is working for the Russians."

He heard the words, but they didn't make any sense at all. They were unintelligible, crazy.

She talked then, the words spilling out, and he listened, and the happiness that he'd carried with him withered like tender shoots yanked from the ground and flung down to die.

At one point, he signaled and crossed the lanes and took the exit to a shopping complex and pulled into the parking lot. When he stopped the car, he turned to face her.

He raised an eyebrow. "So you thought I was on the take?"

He spoke quietly enough, but her face flushed a dull red.

"I didn't know you."

He nodded at that.

"You got to know me pretty damned quick, didn't you?"

He didn't want to look in her eyes. They looked anguished, but she was an actress, wasn't she? "So it was all a lie, right from the first. The aspiring writer, the young lady who couldn't swim very well. Are you a good swimmer?"

She swallowed. "Yes."

"A good swimmer. An actress. Yes, I'd say you're a damn good actress. Meryl Streep couldn't have done it any better. Did it amuse you that I fell for you so quickly, was that fun?"

"Jake, please …"

"Jake, please what? Do you want me to clap now?"

It was ugly. He knew it was ugly, but his heart was breaking, the heart he'd controlled for so long, it was breaking into tiny dry pieces like shattered glass.

Tears glistened in her eyes. One hand rose and reached out to him and it made his heart ache another way. She looked so weary, so vulnerable and there were dark, bruised shadows beneath her eyes. He wanted to hold her and comfort her and he fought against it. Didn't he have any pride? Was he a man or not? Well, he knew the answer to that one. He might be a fool once, but not twice, no by God, not twice. So she'd come onto him for an FBI set up. The anger throbbed in his mind and he remembered her opening words, somebody on his staff, but what the hell did that have to do with an FBI sting? A goddamn setup.

"So your job was to attract me?" He laughed and it was a harsh, unpleasant sound. "You did an A-number-one job, didn't you?"

"Jake, you've got to listen to me."

"I've heard enough." He rasped out the words. "God knows I've heard enough. So what's the point in telling me? Are you trying a little blackmail? I know the FBI doesn't have anything on me, lady, because I don't take bribes. But so you want a few thousand or you'll feed the story to the gossip tabloids. Well, I can tell you …"

She did reach out now and her hand clung to his arm and she was shaking his arm and tears streamed down her face. "You've got to listen to me, you've got to. It isn't the FBI, it's the Russians."

The words finally pierced the haze of anger and he felt like he'd been kicked in the chest. He stared at her.

"The Russians …"

He listened in shock as she told him the rest of it, how she'd decided to go ahead and photograph his safe because that would prove his innocence, and how she'd driven to Los Angeles and gone to the FBI office and the agent named Ellis Kemp wasn't the man who hired her, her shock, and her decision to go to the meeting in San Francisco and follow the contact and how she'd done that and the trail ended at the Russian consulate, and how she'd started back to Carmel determined to get the compact camera and the key to the safe, and how a black Ford pickup tried to ram her off the road.

"For Christ's sake …" He could see it all, imagine what could have happened, the red Porsche hurtling through the air, twisting and turning, to smash on the rocks. She'd survived through nerve and skill and bravery and the quick raw red hurt of anger began to dissolve and he felt again an urge to comfort her, to hold her in his arms and protect her. What a hell of a woman she was. Now she looked like a lost child, exhausted and driven, but still she talked, looking him squarely in the eye, telling him without fanfare or histrionics what she'd done and how. And she was overwhelmingly right on one score, he did have to listen. This was important, more important than wounded feelings, more important than his career, more important than his faith in his staff or his shock at what she'd disclosed.

Whether she'd told him all the truth or not, she was telling him someone had access to his safe and that safe had recently held very important papers, the complete specifications of the United States' latest and newest and most important missile for attacking enemy aircraft, the country's foremost line of defense against a surprise attack.

He turned on the motor, jerked the car into gear and accelerated. There was no time to lose.

Kirsten felt empty. He was furiously angry, she could tell it in his barbed comments, see it in the taut set of his mouth, but she had told him, she had done her best, she'd reached the end of the road. What happened now was out of her hands. She was powerless now to reach him, to change the reality of what had happened.

She was too bereft to cry. Her pain was beyond tears. She'd entered into a play and found the only reality of her life. Today she had killed her present, her future.

She leaned back in the seat and turned her face to watch him. He was the most compelling man she'd ever met. She would have lived and died for him if she could have had the chance. She would have spent her life trying to please him and care for him and now that possibility was gone forever.

He was driving too fast. The scenery was just a blur, but he knew the urgency of her information. At least, he'd accepted that. Soon enough they would be talking to officials, to the CIA. She would have to go over and over it, but the search would be set in motion. When she'd told them what she knew, and then it would all be over for her. She would never see him again.

She didn't have to ask when they reached their destination, an enormous sprawling complex of buildings. Even on Sunday, there were guards to pass, but soon enough they plunged into a labyrinth of corridors, their heels clicking hollowly down a deserted hallway. They paused, and the man who led them unlocked a door midway down a long hall, clicked on the lights, and stood aside for them to enter.

"If you'll be seated, Mr. Connor will be with you in just a few minutes.

Jake sat down at the head of the long conference table. He ignored Kirsten.

Kirsten stood uncertainly just inside the door. The bare and utilitarian room daunted her. A single conference table with chairs at each end and three chairs on each side. No windows, no decoration, nothing but bare plastered walls painted a light gray and a dull, pseudo-marble floor.

"You might as well sit down."

He could have been speaking to a total stranger. No, his voice would have been more polite if she had been a stranger.

Kirsten didn't answer. Instead, she stood stubbornly by the door. She would do what she had to do, then she would leave all of this behind her, go home. Was that tiny, empty, now dusty apartment in Huntington Beach home? She felt suddenly alone and desolate, nothing ahead of her, everything she'd hoped for behind her. She looked across the small room at Jake, but he might as well have been on another planet. He sat at the end of the table, his face impassive, his eyes cold, and she wanted to cry out, "Don't you remember ..."

The door opened. Two men came in. The one in the lead was chunky, an old football player, with massive shoulders and hands and a full fleshy face. He moved briskly toward Jake, ignoring her, and held out his hand. "Sam Connor." Then he introduced his companion, "Mark Rizzo."

No one looked at her.

Connor plunged right in. "I understand you have a security problem, Senator."

Jake didn't waste time. He outlined everything Kirsten had told him, reducing it to a handful of crisp, unemotional sentences.

The three men turned and looked at her.

For an instant, Kirsten had trouble breathing, then slowly she nodded.

"Please be seated, Miss Soderstrom."

It was a command, not a request.

Connor began genially, but his small, pig-like eyes were cold. "You know we appreciate the help of all citizens in matters such as this. I would like to make it clear that you are entitled to counsel if you wish and that any statements you make may later be presented in a court of law."

Kirsten stared at him in disbelief. Did they think she was part of the conspiracy? But hadn't she made it clear that she'd stumbled into this innocently?

Then the nightmare began as question followed question, sometimes the same question in slightly different form, sometimes new questions ("What was the man wearing at the casting agency, Miss Soderstrom?" "Could you read the license plate numbers of the black Ford pickup that you claim tried to force you off the road?" "Oh, you couldn't?" "Are you sure you've never worked for a foreign intelligence service, perhaps when you were in college?")

Connor asked the questions, rapidly, forcefully. Rizzo ran the tape recorder. They were polite, but the questions went on and on and Kirsten's head began to ache and she was thirsty. They brought her water and, later, someone brought in sandwiches and coffee, but the questions went on and on.

She exploded once.

"But I've told you and told you, and I can't tell it any other way because that's just the way it happened. I didn't know these people were Russian agents. For God's sake, if I hadn't told the Senator no one would know and they would be getting away with it so why do you go on and on at me?"

"Now, Miss Soderstrom," Connor said soothingly, "You misunderstand us, but you want us to get to the bottom of this, I know you do, and we really need your help. If you can just tell us again about the phone call last night when you talked to 'Mr. Kemp' in your apartment at Carmel ..."

Kirsten told it again but now her voice was a halting monotone. She wasn't sure when she realized they thought she was lying because their faces never changed nor the tone of their voices, but the questions went on and on and when she changed a word or forgot for a moment, she sensed their eagerness, the eagerness of the hunter when the wounded prey stumbles.

Kirsten moved restlessly in her chair and looked down the long table at Jake, but he sat with his chin cupped in his hand, staring down at a legal pad. If only he would look up. Surely he knew she was telling the truth about her involvement with the Russians. She expected and understood his anger over their contrived meeting and her lies about being an actress, but surely he knew she wasn't a traitor.

He looked up and his eyes were those of a stranger, cool, disinterested, aloof.

Kirsten slumped in her chair. She was tired, terribly tired, and she felt bruised and buffeted. In her heart, she'd known Jake would be angry. She had expected it, had girded herself for the pain, but that didn't help. Knowing you were going to suffer didn't make suffering any easier, but she'd been sure in her heart that once she reached the CIA she would then be able to convince him she'd meant well and always wanted to do the best thing for him. Now, there was a welling sense of fear because they distrusted her. That was it, they distrusted her, but why did they think she'd started the whole thing by telling Jake ...

She didn't understand the question at first. She shook her head slowly. Her head throbbed and there was a dull ache behind her eyes. Her tongue felt thick. "I don't understand." She stared across the table at Connor.

He repeated the question. "When did you decide to double-cross the KGB, Miss Soderstrom?"

Kirsten never knew where she found the strength or the courage. Slowly, she pushed back the straight chair and stood to her full height of five foot seven inches. She held her head up despite the numbing fatigue.

"I'm not the one." She said it distinctly in a voice that could carry to the last row in a theater. Then she looked past Connor to Jake. "Don't you believe me either?" Her voice broke a little. "I give you my word, Jake. Once I knew you, I never believed for an instant that you could be dishonest, ever, about anything. I searched the safe because I was so certain I wouldn't find money there. I went to Los Angeles to face the FBI directly, and that's when I realized it was a lie, the whole story of the sting. I was going to tell you as soon as I got back to Carmel but you'd already left for Washington. I swear this is true. I swear it."

It was very silent in the bare, gray-walled room. Then Jake Johnson, slowly, wearily, began to clap.

When the spasmodic, echoing sound trailed off to nothingness, Connor said emphatically, "Did you decide to come up with this story when you realized you might have a chance to hook the Senator?"

Kirsten attacked. "What good does it do me to reveal all this? If I'd wanted to hold onto the Senator, I could just have kept quiet and,"

"We will know if a copy of the papers in his safe shows up in Moscow. Don't kid yourself. We'll know." He paused and smiled grimly. "I'm sure you do know that, and you also know that we would look immediately at people who could have had access to that safe. Including any recent additions to the Senator's circle. You would be the obvious suspect, Miss Soderstrom. The members of his staff have been with him for years. No, you took on a job, then you saw a better future as Mrs. Jacob Johnson and ..."

Jake moved at that, stood up and leaned forward. "All right, you've got her story. I don't want to hear any more of this. You can get in touch with me and …"

"Wait a minute, Senator, hold on just a minute." Connor was polite, but insistent.

Jake paused, his face set and determined.

"Now as I understand it, Senator, the original plan was for you to pick Miss Soderstrom up at the airport and take her to your home in Virginia to be your guest."

"That was the plan."

"We'd better stick to it, Senator."

"Oh no," Jake retorted. "Absolutely not. She and I are going our separate ways, Mr. Connor."

Slowly, the CIA agent shook his head.

"Think about it, Senator. Don't you see? She's our only link with the Russians. According to her, they're going to set up a meeting to retrieve the camera and the key. If that's true, they don't know she's been singing to us, and we can't afford for them to realize it. They might drop her altogether. So you and Miss Soderstrom are going to have to be very good friends for at least a while longer."

13

KIRSTEN WAS INTENSELY AWARE of Jake's nearness, but he might as well have been in Timbuctoo as within reach in the driver's seat of the MG. As he whirled the car off the main highway and onto a narrow blacktop, she said sharply, "I don't want to do this either."

He made no reply, looking stonily ahead. The country road curved up and downhill, and the enormous trees pressed close. It would be spectacularly lovely in the autumn with the red and gold of sumac and oak and maple. The serenity of the wooded hillsides was in stark contrast to the tension between them.

Then, with no explanation, Jake braked the car and eased it to a stop. They were on top of a ridge. Ahead of them, the road plunged down into a valley then climbed again. On the opposite side, the western sun gilded a Greek Revival mansion. Immense white pillars supported its two-story portico. It was built of brick that had faded to a dusty rose over the years. It dominated the ridge, and Kirsten knew this must be Jake's home.

Slowly, she turned and looked at him and he was watching her, his eyes dark with pain.

"I don't think I can do it," he said roughly.

"We don't have any choice. You'll find out, all of you," she said bitterly, "when this is through, that I have told you the truth."

"I would like to believe you," he said slowly, "but you are an actress."

"Yes, I am an actress, but being an actress doesn't mean that my every word and gesture are contrived and artificial. Surely you can see that. Surely you understand what is real and what isn't real."

"I just don't know ..." He rubbed his cheek. "You told me you wanted to write scripts, you convinced me of that."

"That's true and I'd never told anyone before you."

"You really do want to write scripts?"

"Yes," she said eagerly. "I want to write and act and I know I can do it."

"Is your name really Kirsten Soderstrom and you went to Vassar?"

Tears glistened in her eyes. "Yes, I am Kirsten Soderstrom and I went to Vassar – on scholarship."

"Why do you make that so clear?"

"Because I want you to understand that I'm not the kind of girl you've always known. I may have gone to Vassar but I went as a poor girl. I'm not a deb."

"Why do you think that's important to me?"

She hated to bring it back to the beginning, but she had to. "That was in the prep book they gave me. It had all kinds of personal information about you, that you liked rich girls, and you liked blondes."

He reached out and touched her hair very lightly, then pulled his hand away.

"This material that they gave you to study, it was all about me?"

For the first time in hours, he didn't sound angry. Instead, he looked at her thoughtfully.

Kirsten nodded.

"Do you still have it?"

"No. I was instructed to learn it then I returned it when I met the woman at the Huntington galleries."

He thought about that for a moment then he looked at her searchingly. "Tell me everything in it, every last detail you can remember."

Kirsten closed her eyes briefly, then began. She had a good memory. She was a quick memorizer. Once she got a script down, she rarely forgot a line. She knew she was repeating the report almost verbatim, and an occasional skillful question from Jake brought forth even the most minute of details.

He interrupted once. "Say that again."

"The report said," she continued carefully, precisely, "that you were very bitter about the failure of your marriage, that you attributed it to Francesca being an actress and that you were very scornful of people who earned their living by playing charades."

"God almighty," he said. Then, slowly, he looked at her and Kirsten couldn't understand the expression on his face, a mixture of shock and sorrow and anger … and something more.

She waited, not understanding and not daring to hope.

He stared across the valley at the house high on the ridge, but Kirsten didn't know what he saw or what he thought. He looked angry again now, angry and very determined.

He faced her, "I'd better explain my household to you. My housekeeper is Mrs. Parker. She's about fifty and she's been with me for a good many years. You know Drew and Amy and Murray."

She looked at him in surprise. "Do they live with you?"

"Yes, I suppose that's a little out of the ordinary, but it just kind of happened. Drew and Amy already worked for me before I was elected so, when I came to Washington and found the house, they stayed with me. Somehow, there never seemed any real reason for them to move out, and Amy enjoyed acting as my hostess. After all, I've got plenty of room."

Kirsten looked again at the mansion. Yes, it would have plenty of room.

"Drew hates to be out a penny." Jake shook his head. "He's probably got the first nickel he ever made. He just kind of moved in. As for Murray, well, Murray's been with me since the war."

Kirsten took a deep breath and stared at the house and now it didn't look so friendly, it merely looked big and imposing and strange, and it harbored all of them, Amy and Drew and Murray.

Then she realized Jake was talking to her and his words shocked her.

"All right, Kirsten. You and I are supposed to be lovers. Right?"

She hated hearing him say it in such a businesslike tone, but she would have to get used to it. The bond that had been growing between them was dead now, destroyed. It was purely a business proposition from now on. For an instant she wondered if she could bear it, but she had no choice. Whether Jake or the CIA agents believed her was beside the point. She knew that she was telling the truth and that meant she was the only person in the world who knew, beyond any shadow of a doubt, that someone on Jake's staff was a traitor. Only if she continued and helped the CIA find the people who had hired her could she set them on the right trail that ultimately would lead back to Jake's office.

Despite the harrowing disclosures of the day, he looked strong and determined and she loved the firm line of his mouth and the hawk-like intensity of his eyes. He was wonderful and, even if she wouldn't win his love, she could help him, and she would do it no matter how hard it might be.

She managed a small smile. "That's the script, Jake."

"Then if anyone's watching us park on this ridge, we shouldn't disappoint them."

She found it hard to breathe as his arm slipped around her shoulders and he brought his face close to hers.

When his lips touched hers, she knew with sudden certainty that he still desired her, no matter how he felt about her actions. For an instant, she resisted. What kind of basis was that for making love? But even as she thought it, her hands pulled his head down closer and she kissed him in return, a full, exciting, promising kiss, and she didn't care about right or wrong or the future or the past— all that mattered was the moment and his nearness and the rush of desire that threatened to sweep her far beyond any bounds of propriety.

Abruptly, he pulled back. "Kirsten ..." he stopped and shook his head. "We'd better go in."

Murray was waiting for them in the circle drive. He opened the car door for her and reached a hand to help her out. Kirsten smiled her thanks, but it took all of her control not to shrink from his touch. When he turned to get her suitcase, she stared at him. What did her instinct tell her? Was it only that he was different? She knew well enough the human tendency to fear the strange, and Murray was strange, his great size, the emptiness of his face, his rarity of speech. Or was her instinct warning her, saying here is the one who is dangerous?

Drew called out as he sauntered toward the railing of the second-story portico, "We were about to send out the Mounties."

"We had to do a little sightseeing first," Jake replied easily.

Kirsten felt a moment of shock. Jake's manner was perfect. He was the comfortable host, the relaxed and debonair senator taking a well-earned afternoon of leisure. For a moment, she couldn't believe what she was hearing. Then he turned and took her arm and they started up the broad white steps and she knew that it was her turn to act and, for the first time in her life, she wondered if she could.

Amy Montgomery stood in the open doorway, not quite a hostess giving a welcome but very close to it. Kirsten wondered what Amy's thoughts were as she smiled down at them. Did she see Kirsten as an interloper? Did she fear for her position as de facto hostess for Senator Jacob Holland Johnson? And how could any woman live in the same house with Jake and not be attracted to him?

"Welcome to Markwood Hall. We were afraid you'd missed your flight or something equally dire," Drew called down.

Kirsten looked up. Drew was shading his eyes against the sun so it was hard to see his face, but she thought his words very revealing. Wasn't there a school of thought that insisted that all comments laughingly made revealed innermost desires? Had Drew really not wanted her to arrive?

Kirsten stopped short on the steps. She felt surrounded by enmity, threatened, endangered.

Jake's hand touched her arm, gave her a solid, reassuring squeeze as if to say, "Come on, Kirsten, it's all right, I'm here and we can do this together." But that couldn't be right. He was angry with her, wasn't he? She was bewildered, but the strong touch of his hand was there and real. She felt immeasurably strengthened. She lifted her head and smiled up at Drew, then nodded to Amy and said, "It's wonderful to be here," and her voice was clear and vibrant and strong.

She moved on up the steps, Jake beside her, and wished it all could have been different, that she and Jake could be the way they'd been in Carmel.

Kirsten wore a pale ivory silk dress down to dinner. As she walked down the curving staircase she was struck again by the grace and beauty of the house. The lower hall was in the Federal period with pillars supporting the curved ceiling with its detailed plaster work including a central medallion that provided an ornate backdrop for the double-tiered crystal chandelier. A Chippendale table and a fine gilt mirror stood by the entrance to the living room. She paused in the doorway and saw Jake standing with his back to her by the Georgian wood mantel. He wore a soft tweed jacket and gray slacks and looked perfectly at home in the dignified room with its pale gray-green walls and oyster-white curtains. A Hepplewhite armchair sat by a secretary-bookcase filled with English porcelains. A Persian rug, a muted blue-green, covered most of the hand-pegged flooring. The other chairs and couches in the room were antique, too, yet the final effect was one of comfort and ease. It was a room where people lived, and the lovely works of art were both functional and decorative.

Jake turned then and saw her and hurried across the room, his hands reaching out to hers. Once again, she felt a wash of surprise then a passionate wish that this could be real, that this weren't merely for effect. She realized as he took her hands and drew her close that Amy was walking into the room behind her and Kirsten knew he was only keeping up the charade – and he hated charades.

Jake bent close. "Smile, Kirsten."

She did smile but her heart ached, and throughout dinner, despite the easy, good-humored conversation, she felt a current of tension, but wondered whether it emanated from her. Once again, she marveled at Jake's composure and tried to match it.

The dining room was spectacular, too, with the same immensely tall ceilings and dramatically large windows as in the living room. The walls were powder-blue and delicate off-white stucco decorations festooned the walls above the tall windows.

Conversation ranged from the prospects for an oil shortage if Iran blocked the Straits of Hormuz, to the need for stiffer penalties for computer hacking, to the difficulties of keeping a clay court in prime condition.

Amy looked bored when Jake and Drew soberly assessed the effects of an oil shortage, but she brightened and talked animatedly about the tennis court.

"Is tennis one of your passions, Amy?" Kirsten asked lightly.

"Amy is passionate about every inch of Markwood Hall," Drew replied.

The light died out of Amy's eyes and she seemed to draw into herself, and her cameo-smooth face was unreadable.

Did she also care passionately for the master of Markwood Hall? Could she be bitter that Jake didn't look at her, had never expressed an interest in her? Could gratitude for his help after her husband's death be mixed with resentment that Jake lived and prospered and her husband was dead these many years?

Now Amy sat subdued, a self-effacing secretary, easy to overlook. Could Amy be the one?

Then Kirsten turned to Drew. He sat at ease after dinner was over, drinking strong black coffee and smoking an after-dinner cigar. What motivated Drew?

"Tell me about yourself," Kirsten said smilingly,

Drew blew a perfect smoke ring, one and then another, and said lightly, "I'm not an after-dinner speaker, Kirsten. The senator's your man."

"But I know all about him."

Drew cocked his head at that. "Do you now? I'll bet you didn't know he loves pistachio nuts but hates almonds?"

"I bow to you superior knowledge," Kirsten rejoined.

"Do you know his favorite game?" Amy asked, and there was sudden animation in her face.

Kirsten knew that Amy was delighted to have an opportunity to display how much better she knew Jake and Kirsten once again felt a rush of jealousy, but she managed a smile and said lightly, "I'm afraid not."

"He loves Trivial Pursuit, and he can't bear charades."

Kirsten was looking at Jake as Amy spoke. He was smiling. He continued to smile, but his eyes were suddenly unreadable, opaque.

There was an instant's pause that to Kirsten seemed freighted with intensity; then, as quickly as it had come, the feeling passed, and Jake was laughing, "I will confess to being an open book, which I'm sure would please my constituents."

"Now that's a lie, Senator," Drew said quickly. "You have a singularly Byzantine mind, characterized by an inordinate amount of craft and guile."

"Ah, to see ourselves as others see us. But I believe we've revealed enough about me to our guest. How about a game of Trivial Pursuit?"

They settled in the card room and the battle continued for several hours. Kirsten and Jake paired against Amy and Drew. There were hotly contested questions and anguished moans over mistakes quickly realized. The advantage seesawed back and forth and, once, Drew and Amy were a question away from winning but faltered on the easternmost point in the contiguous United States. Three turns later, Kirsten and Jake correctly identified the disease *la rage* as rabies and swept to victory, exuding self-satisfaction.

Drew stretched and yawned. "I don't believe I've ever had the pleasure of facing such odious winners."

"That's sour grapes if I've ever heard them," Jake retorted. He stood, too. "Nightcap anyone?"

Kirsten shook her head and looked away from him. When the game started, she'd seen Amy and Drew exchange a surprised glance. That glance would have embarrassed her once, for it said as plainly as a question, *hey, what goes here, aren't they in love, what's this game stuff?* But she'd pushed that thought way down deep and now, once again, it was clear that Jake was delaying the goodnights, dragging out the evening. All right, let him, she'd expected nothing more, but she had thought their plan was to keep up the pretense. Suddenly, she was so tired, too tired to stay in the room another minute.

Jake was pouring scotch into a glass and adding soda and ice when she stood.

"I believe I'll say goodnight now. I enjoyed the game."

The others smiled and said goodnight and she walked out of the cardroom and up the stairs and tried not to think of what this night could have been like if she and Jake were lovers still. Once in her room, she looked slowly around. It was a beautiful room with the soft apricot of the walls repeated in the Aubusson rug and again in the drapes. She saw her own reflection in the full-length mirror that hung beside an old oak dresser. The glass was smoky with age and her image was indistinct, ghostlike.

Kirsten sighed and walked to the dresser. She opened the drawers and found her few things which she had brought with her. Obviously, Markwood Hall was well run. Everything was done for the guest's convenience. The bed was turned down, a carafe of ice water sat on a bedside table. But there was no provision for a broken heart.

14

KIRSTEN KNEW THE PEACH nightgown was flattering. The neckline dipped in front, emphasizing the fullness of her breasts, and the gown fit smoothly over her hips and legs, but it scarcely mattered. No one was going to see her in the gown.

She heard the others come upstairs and final laughing goodnights and the slam of the door next to her room and she knew that was Jake's room.

Kirsten knew she should go to bed. She'd had very little sleep, only the few hours on the flight from Los Angeles to Washington, then she'd undergone the trauma of telling Jake and the hostility of the CIA agents and, finally, the long evening at Markwood Hall which only emphasized her distance from Jake. She should go to bed, but she stood in the center of the room and listened to the occasional movement in the room next to hers and hungered to see him. More than that, she hungered to love him, to know him, to feel his body next to hers.

He had kissed her that afternoon when they stopped on the ridge and the magic was still there for both of them, she had no doubt of that, but the barrier was up between them tonight. He smiled and he played at being a lover, but only because the CIA had insisted.

He still desired her, she knew that, clung to it, but did she want him on those terms?

She took a deep breath. She wanted him on any terms at all. She had no pride where Jake was concerned. If she loved him, perhaps he would know then, would recognize deep inside that this couldn't be acting, this couldn't be anything but love.

Moving quickly now, she snatched up her negligee and slipped it on and opened her door.

Jake stripped down to his shorts and walked to the chair by the fireplace. He carried his drink with him. He needed to think and he needed to think damn hard. He'd sworn a long time ago, while the hurt from Francesca still festered, that he would never get involved, ever again, with an actress. Was that why he'd been so angry this afternoon when Kirsten told him? He couldn't blame her for believing that a sting was underway. Hell, they happened all the time and caught up lots of legislators. She didn't know him, so that was all right, though he would hope his public projection came over a little more solidly than that. Still, that was understandable.

What he hated was the fact that she was an actress and that their first meeting was contrived and he'd fallen hard, very hard. He'd thought she was a miracle and he'd given up believing in miracles.

Did she have sex with him because she was playing a part for the FBI?

His heart rejected it, absolutely, completely, totally.

Jake took a deep swallow of the scotch but scarcely noticed the smooth, smoky flavor.

Look at it – if Kirsten were telling the truth, the entire truth, then there was something very rotten close to him – and one fact tipped the scale in her favor. She'd described the report on him that she'd studied which contained the statement that he hated people who made their living by playing charades. He remembered the day he said that and he'd said it only once, one morning on the way into the District. Murray was driving the car and he was talking to Amy and Drew.

Jake finished the drink and pushed restlessly up from his chair and paced to the window and looked out into the darkness.

One of them could have repeated it, but that would be odd. It wasn't an appropriate comment for a Senator from the state of California and Amy and Drew were political animals. They knew what could be quoted and what couldn't. Murray, well, the idea that he would have repeated any comment was absurd.

There were other pointers, too, including the timing. He'd decided only the week before that he would steal away to California, for a few days. He made that decision and arranged on the same day for Amy and Drew to announce he would be in New York and also requested that the Amraam material be delivered to California by military courier.

Someone moved fast, putting the ad in the Hollywood Reporter, hiring Kirsten, and having her arrive in Carmel the very day the Amraam material came in. The execution fast, professional, and very, very neat.

How in the hell could it have been done without the connivance of either Amy or Drew? Or Murray? He had to add him.

Connor, that CIA agent, didn't believe Kirsten's claim she'd thought she was working for the FBI. Connor thought she was a willing recruit to the KGB who'd changed her mind when she realized she'd attracted Jake's attention.

Jake pounded his fist once hard against the well. Dammit, he didn't know. How could he know? She was bewitchingly lovely. He felt complete when she was near. How could he know?

The knock at his door was soft and hesitant. He turned slowly and looked at the door. The handle moved. The door swung in. Kirsten stood framed in the doorway.

He watched her. His is eyes devoured her. He felt the same magic whenever she entered a room, the same sweep of enchantment. She was stunningly, breathtakingly lovely. Now instead of sunlight, the soft glow from the chandelier made her ash blonde hair glisten and emphasized the deep violet of her eyes, the delicate, fine bones of her face. She stood in the doorway and her soft cream negligee swirled around her figure. He glimpsed the fullness of her breasts curving beneath the peach gown and he felt the beginning throb of desire mixing with a glorious wonder at her presence.

She stepped inside the room and slowly the door closed behind her.

"Jake."

Her voice was husky and there was a plea in it.

Slowly, he walked across the room until he stood looking down at her, and suddenly, deep within him, there was a sense of coming home, of rightness. It wasn't a matter of logic or reason.

"I believe you."

Kirsten felt as though an immeasurable weight had rolled away from him.

"Oh Jake, Jake, Jake," and she flung her arms around him and he felt the soft warmth of her face against his chest and felt, too, the welling up a happiness that went far beyond reason.

When she looked up at him with a smile that lifted his heart he said slowly, "If I can't believe in you, I can't believe in anything."

Kirsten reached up and framed his face in her hands. She looked deeply into his eyes, dear, dark warm eyes, eyes that told her of love and trust. She felt as though she'd come from the depths of despair to the heights of joy, all, because this man cared for her. Her life could never be the same. She would always care more for him than for herself. She would never again be free of worry and concern because his welfare would be paramount. Whatever happened to her life, be it good or bad, depended upon him. It was both a wonderful and a fearful understanding, but she would never willingly trade for her days of independence because that was just another way of saying that she was living a life without love. Love was worth every toll it exacted.

"Jake, I promise you," she said softly, "I will love you with all my heart and soul for all of my life."

"And I will love you with all my heart and soul for all of my life," he repeated softly.

They stood in each other's arms. Peace and joy cradled them, held them in a glow of delight.

Jake bent his head and their lips touched and they kissed gently at first until the fire of desire flamed within them. He swept her off her feet and carried her to his bed.

When they were lying together, he smiled at her and his fingers gently touched the line of her cheek and throat and then his hands caressed her and all the while his eyes looked deeply into hers and she welcomed his touch. As moments passed, all thought was lost in feeling and the glory of coming together.

When their breathing quieted, Kirsten pulled up on an elbow and looked down into his dark, relaxed face. She felt a rush of wonder. She had thought love was foreclosed forever and it wasn't. Jake believed in her, trusted her, loved her. Quickly, she leaned down and kissed the corner of his mouth.

Then the happiness seeped out of her face because he was frowning.

Her voice was small. "What's wrong?"

He wasn't looking at her. His brows were drawn in a tight frown and his face looked suddenly hard. "I don't like it."

Somehow she managed to ask him. "What do you mean?"

He looked at her moved quickly, crooking an arm around her neck, pulling her down into the circle of his arms, squeezing her against him. "Not us, love. Don't look like that, Kirsten. I'm talking about the plan to have you meet the Russians."

"Oh, that." She dismissed it. "That's all right. I mean, what else can we do?"

"I don't know," he said slowly. He turned and plumped the pillows up and pulled her up with him to sit back against them. "I do know. We can look harder for the original leak." Once again he frowned.

Kirsten understood this frown. "I'm sorry."

He reached for her hand. She knew he was holding onto her because he was looking at betrayal by someone close to him. If he had found commitment with her, he had at the same time lost faith in his staff or at least in one member of his staff.

"Jake, don't you see, as soon as the Russians get in touch with me and set up a meeting, that will be the beginning of the end of all this. Once the CIA discovers who contacted me, they can go back over that person's past and find out which one of your staff members he knows."

Jake was somber. "I have a feeling it's going to be a hard path to trace. Whoever set this up is clever, clever and careful. I wish you weren't going to be involved."

"I don't mind, especially if it helps clear it all up. In fact, I'm looking forward to it," she said determinedly. "I haven't forgotten the pickup that tried to shove me off the road. I feel like 'Mr. Kemp' and I have a score to settle."

Jake reached out then and gripped her wrist. "Do you have any reason to think they may realize you're on to them?"

"They still think I'm the prize chump. You remember, 'Mr. Kemp' called me at the apartment in Carmel. He had no idea I followed the contact to the Consulate. I convinced him I skipped the meeting because someone was following me. He wanted to set up another meeting there but I told him I had to come to Washington. He didn't like that." Kirsten smiled.

"He was mad?"

"Furious."

"I don't like it."

"Serves him right."

"Kirsten, be serious."

"I am serious."

"Not serious enough. These people are dangerous. They tried to run you off the road in California after they thought you'd made contact in San Francisco. What will they try here when you walk into a meeting?"

Some of Kirsten's ebullience faded, but still she felt on top of the world. Jake loved her and believed in her. The CIA might have doubted her, but her word would be proven in the long run. It was going to be alright. She and Jake were going to win.

Jake's eyes were dark with worry, thinking about the pickup. "Why did they want to run you off the road?"

Thinking about the pickup made her feel hollow and sick, but maybe Jake was right. They needed to understand. Kirsten didn't want to think about it because it still made her feel hollow and sick

"I suppose," she began slowly, "that if the papers surface in Moscow and then they could trace back that I had some meetings with a known Russian agent and I wasn't available to talk to, they would decide I was a traitor. I mean, I wouldn't be around to say 'Hey no. I was set up for this.'"

Jake sat bolt upright. The sheet fell down around his waist. He slammed a fist into the opposite palm. "They never intended for you to be able to talk to the CIA." He paused. "Oh, my God."

Kirsten understood suddenly, too. She looked at him in dismay. The hollow feeling expanded. She said quickly, trying to ease the fear in his eyes, "No, Jake, it won't happen. The CIA will be all set up. They won't let anything happen to me."

"You're damn right they won't," and he reached over to the bedside table and yanked up the telephone.

"Wait, wait a minute. Who are you calling?"

He was already dialing. "Connor," he said briefly.

Kirsten reached across him and broke the connection.

"Hey, wait a minute," he said brusquely.

Despite her fear and her further determination that by God she was going to help trap the Russians, she couldn't resist smiling at his outrage. The Senator wasn't accustomed to being thwarted.

"You wait a minute," she said sweetly. "Why are you calling Connor?"

"I won't permit you to be live bait."

He wouldn't permit …

Kirsten was accustomed to making her own decisions, going her own way at the hour of her own choosing, and yet she wasn't angered. His declaration meant he loved her, but if he were going to love her he had to learn that she insisted on participatory democracy.

He glowered and she smiled.

"Kirsten," and there was a rising note of anger in his voice, "you don't understand. Those babies play for keeps. This isn't a damn game."

Her smile faded. She slowly nodded. When she spoke, she spoke seriously. "I know," she said gently. "I'm not a fool. I know it's serious. After all, I almost died on that shore drive, so I know they play for keeps. I play for keeps too. This is serious and it's more important than I am, Jake. There's a secret agent out there someplace who is clever and resourceful enough to get a toe-hold into the staff of a United States senator. If he can do it once, he can do it again. I don't know what kind of difference it makes if the Russians get those plans, but I know there is information worth a lot of lives. If we don't find out who's behind this now, we can be certain other and worse things will happen down the road."

"It doesn't have to be you," he said stubbornly. "A decoy can do it."

She gazed at him soberly. "We can trust the CIA. After all, it won't do them any good to have something happen to me. They want to get to the bottom of this."

"I can't lose you." He gripped her shoulders and stared down into her eyes.

It was a moment such as she'd never before experienced, the rapport between two souls, the openness and honesty that revealed a depth of passion and longing and care.

She would never forget this moment, the strength of his face, his blunt chin and bold nose and firm mouth, and the love and fear in his eyes.

Reaching up, she slipped her hands behind his head and drew his face down to hers.

"Don't be frightened for me or for us. We're going to be together, and we're going to succeed, you and me, now and tomorrow and always, no matter what happens."

Her mouth sought his and she offered herself to him with a vigor and delight born of confidence and joy, and, as they kissed she felt the familiar yet always different pulse of passion. Her lips lightly moved across the angular planes of his face and delighted in the muscular smoothness of his chest and the hard flatness of his stomach. As she caressed him, his hands touched her with a growing urgency and then time lost reality and they were swept together in the flood of desire, a reckless, plunging culmination of sensation.

In a moment, he said, almost plaintively, "You distracted me."

Kirsten propped up on an elbow and smiled down at his bemused face.

"Believe in us. No one's going to take the future away from us."

And if deep inside she fought a kernel of fear she was never going to admit it. After all, the CIA would be there.

15

MICHAEL SWALLOWED QUEASILY AND shook his head when the stewardess offered a drink or coffee. He looked out the window, then quickly stared down at his hands when an enormous, multi-branched prong of lightning split the sky. He hated flying, he'd always hated it. His collar felt tight and he reached up and loosened his necktie. Sweat made his shirt clammy. The plane slipped sideways then bucked upward. It had been that way ever since they left Chicago. He hated flying. If it weren't for that damned girl … He hadn't felt easy about it from the beginning, but it was the only way. They had to have somebody to take the heat when it became clear the papers would only be available during that very short period that the Senator would be in Carmel.

Michael swallowed again. If only the damned plane would stop swooping up and down. His stomach felt wobbly. He glanced down at his watch. Another hour to go before they got to Washington.

He wiped beads of sweat from his upper lip. He had to get this mess straightened out. For one thing, Moscow was going to be very, very unhappy with him if he didn't get the plans to them, and he didn't have the plans. The Senator's staffer had refused, absolutely, to pass along the photocopies until the girl was set up as the patsy. If only she'd followed orders and made contact as she was supposed to in San Francisco then everything would have been perfect. She would have been photographed meeting with Iva and the photo thoughtfully sent to the CIA after she was dead. But, of course, her death had to be an accident and that would have worked beautifully in California with its miles of narrow and twisting coastal roads.

Washington, D.C. was another matter entirely and called for an entirely different approach.

His misery with his anguished stomach subsided as he reviewed a new plan. The scheme was complicated, would take very careful doing, but it would work – and no one would ever doubt her guilt once they had her.

The plane abruptly plummeted downward for an agonizingly long time. Michael's nausea returned in full force. Equally abruptly, the jet leveled out and continued on its way.

He hated planes and he hated traveling, but he had to handle this one himself. He was exposed. No one knew that but him, but he knew. He'd personally recruited the Senator's staffer. If suspicion ever pointed that way, it could lead directly to him, Mikhail Vurenov.

The sudden sickening feeling in his stomach was worse than the airsickness, it was the wash of deadly fear He hadn't permitted himself to think of his real name in years, not since he'd emigrated, supposedly from Czechoslovakia after World War II, entering the United States as a Czech refugee, Michael Vincent. It was criminal folly even to remember that name. He was Michael Vincent, a used car dealer in L.A., for God's sake.

Kirsten woke suddenly, one moment deeply asleep, the other sharply, sentiently awake. Light spilled through the huge double windows opposite the bed. And in the warmth of the August sunlight, the heavy, masculine room with its massive mahogany bed and chest and Morris armchair looked comfortable and welcoming.

She smiled. It was a very welcoming room. She turned to look at Jake who slept face down, a pillow bunched under his arm. His thick black hair curled a little on his neck, and she leaned over and blew softly against his hair and he made a noise and moved in his sleep. Kirsten smoothed her hand across the muscular firmness of his back.

Suddenly, he turned to face her. Dark eyes stared into her own. He reached up and tangled his hand in her hair.

"Yeah, they happen."

She looked at him, startled.

"Miracles," he explained. "Miracles before breakfast. That's what you are."

A welcoming room, that's what she'd felt as she awoke. She leaned down and burrowed her face against his chest. "Before breakfast," she repeated, lightly. "That has a nice ring to it."

He laughed at that and they were in each other's arms and they had time to laugh as they loved and they learned anew that love is a miracle of trust and delight. There was no hurry this fine August morning and they took their time, all their time, and he smoothed her hair and touched her lips and traced the soft contours of her body and she felt the soft ripple of his muscles against her and rose to seek him and then they paused and kissed lightly again. Each time, he caressed her and paused and the pulse of desire flared higher until finally she called out to him urgently and she heard his words of pleasure as they came together in a splendor of delight.

When she was lying at rest in the crook of his arm, he twisted his head a little to smile at her. "You know what this is, don't you?"

"I have a fairly good idea," she said demurely.

He grinned at that. "No, really. This is a honeymoon."

"I believe that's restricted to newlyweds."

"Not at all. It's restricted to true lovers. We just have a little head start. I have every intention of continuing at this pace after we're married, too."

"After we're … "She looked up into his face.

"You will marry me, won't you?" His voice wasn't light now at all.

She could never remember later what she said, but she would never forget the drumbeat of happiness in her heart. At that moment, she would have sworn that fate decreed all good things for them.

Kirsten wore a yellow linen dress down for breakfast. She loved that particular dress. It was the color of buttercups and made her think of spring and wildflowers rippling in a warm April breeze. Jake stood as she approached the glass table sitting beneath an awning on the terrace.

"Do you want coffee first or juice?"

"Hmm, coffee."

He poured her a cup. "Good, we're compatible. I always drink my coffee first."

"Actually," and she spoke very softly, without discernible expression, "coffee is good first thing in the morning but other things can be better," and her eyes smiled at him.

"You're right," he said fervently.

Kirsten stopped at the buffet and selected fresh cantaloupe and a Danish, then joined him. She looked around. "Where's everyone else?"

"I believe we might have been the last ones down."

A tiny blush stained her cheeks. "Do you suppose they ... "and she broke off.

"I do. But who cares?" He reached across the table to take her hand. He turned it over and looked at it and shook his head. "This hand looks a little bare to me."

Kirsten followed his gaze then realized he was holding her ring finger.

"How about we do some shopping today?"

Kirsten turned her hand to hold his and she gave it a hard squeeze, then said abruptly, "Not today."

Jake frowned. "Why not? You committed yourself this morning."

She squeezed his hand again. "Of course I did, but we won't go ring shopping until this is all cleared up."

"Why not?"

Kirsten felt the lightness go out of her face. "The CIA has to clear me before we can get married."

"Nobody has to clear you," he said roughly. "To hell with that."

Tears pricked at her eyes. "I love you," she said steadily. "I will always love you, but I won't marry you while I'm under suspicion."

"They may never really know what happened."

"They will. I believe that." Then said quietly. "I have to believe that."

Sandals clicked on the terrace behind them and Kirsten pulled her hand free and picked up her coffee cup.

Jake looked over her shoulder said softly, imperatively, "Remember, you're very tired today. I'll explain later." Then he was smiling at Amy, "You're a Johnny-come-lately this morning. You've usually been in the office for an hour by the time I get down for breakfast."

Amy yawned. "Do we get R&R after a night of Trivial Pursuit?"

Jake shook his head. "So far as I know, that's not in the job description."

"If we start going on job descriptions, I have several bones to pick."

"Are you exploited?" Kirsten asked lightly.

"I'll say," Amy responded. "But I'm going to wait until just before the re-election campaign, then I intend to hit the boss up for a big raise."

Jake laughed good-naturedly. "That's one of the reasons I hired Amy. She can think."

They continued to joke. Kirsten listened with a smile, but, once again, she wondered, *Is there anything that reveals people more than what they choose to joke about?*

As Kirsten finished her sweet roll, she considered Amy and Drew and Murray. She could see Murray leaning up against the low wall that separated the terrace form the rose garden.

When Jake picked up The Post and began to read the front section, Kirsten turned to Amy. She tried to keep her tone casual as she nodded toward the other end of the terrace. "What's Murray doing?"

Amy didn't even look around. "Waiting for his master."

"Does he always lurk near Jake?"

Something flickered in Amy's misty green eyes. "Actually, that's part of his job description. Being a senator has a lot of perks, but it has drawbacks, too, like crazy people with guns who don't like a particular vote." Amy took the last bite of her grapefruit. "One nut tried to shoot Jake last year at a rally in Sonoma, and Murray took it pretty seriously."

Kirsten looked sharply at Amy, but she was carefully edging out her last grapefruit segment. Kirsten felt a throb of anger. How could Amy talk about a threat to Jake calmly, as if she were reading a weather report? She was talking about Jake's life.

Amy continued placidly, "So Murray watches."

Kirsten looked again at the hulking figure leaning against the low wall. Now he looked benign, not sinister.

Amy reached for a section of newspaper and soon she, too, was absorbed. Kirsten sat, her roll half eaten, and looked thoughtfully down at the rose gardens. With all the concerns she'd battled these last few days, it had never occurred to her to be worried about Jake's safety. She'd grown up knowing about that kind of fear. A prosecutor's daughter learns early on of death threats. One frightful day a radio bulletin announced an escaped killer was gunning for her father. She never forgot the terrible anxiety as she'd hurried downtown to his office and her relief at finding him safe. She'd begged her father to quit, to go into private practice, but he shook his head and said quietly, "I'll do what I think is right, Kirsten, and trust in God."

She looked across the table as Jake put down the paper. Loving him was going to take a particular kind of courage. She hoped she could measure up.

He glanced up and saw her eyes on him and his face lighted, sweeping away the darkness in her heart. Whatever the cost, loving him was worth any price.

"Kirsten, let's walk in the garden." As he stood and helped pull back her chair, he said briskly to Amy, "We'll go into the District, after all. Kirsten's ragged out from her trip and wants to rest up so I have a couple of projects for us to take care of."

Amy nodded. "Do you want Drew, too?"

"Yes. Round him up and tell Murray to have the car ready in half an hour."

Amy moved toward the house as Jake pulled open the low gate for Kirsten.

When they were some yards down the curving path, Kirsten asked, "Why am I tired?"

"Because I think it's time we did some looking around." Then he grimaced. "I don't like to ask you to do it, but I don't see another way."

He waited until they were on the bridge that spanned the pond to tell Kirsten his plan. It was incongruous to make plans such as these in the midst of the serenity and quiet of the lush Virginia countryside, but she and Jake were not private individuals who could live and love freely. They were involved in an intricate maneuver designed by others. So far, they were blocked. Any move would be better than none.

Kirsten bid the others good morning and walked upstairs, ostensibly to rest, but in her room she paced back and forth. Her hands were moist and she rubbed them several times on her cotton slacks. She'd told Jake she didn't mind at all, but now that the moment was at hand she felt a stirring of panic that she sternly quelled. This was her chance to do something to help. She would do what he asked, no matter how distasteful it might be.

The throaty murmur of the diesel Mercedes wafted up from the drive. Kirsten moved to the window, stood to one side, and looked down. Jake and Amy got in the back seat. Drew joined Murray in the front. The car moved smoothly down the drive, picking up speed.

Kirsten moved quickly to the door, opened it. She stood in the hall, listening. A vacuum cleaner buzzed downstairs. She looked up and down the hall, but no one moved in the quiet. She walked across the landing. After one more quick glance up and down the hall, she opened the second door and stepped inside. She paused long enough to be certain no one was in the room. The bed was made, so the maid had already seen to Amy's room.

Kirsten closed the door and waited a moment for her breathing to ease, then looked slowly around the room. She had never in her life pried in another person's bedroom, but these were not normal circumstances.

She felt chilled when she studied the room, because it was impersonal, yet this was Amy's home. She had her own room and sitting room and bath and even a tiny office off the sitting room.

Kirsten didn't know what she was looking for, but for anything that wouldn't accord with Amy's public face. Amy was the quintessential secretary, pleasant, self-effacing, agreeable.

What lay behind her cameo-smooth face? What did she think and feel? Did she care for Jake, either as a friend or more than that? Was she resentful of him? Could she, would she work to injure him? Was there any way a KGB operative could have gained her trust?

The walls were a pale, cool green, the curtains a crisp white. The bed and chest were English Chippendale, elegant yet austere. Two paintings hung in the room and both were of the crashing surf on the Big Sur. There was a sense of space and distance, of calmness and order.

This was not the room of an emotionally open person. This was the room of a contained and controlled individual. There were no knickknacks, no Dresden or porcelain figures, and no souvenirs, nothing to hint at Amy's passions or appetites.

Kirsten crossed to the chest that was as neat and bare as everything in the room except for a single photograph in a silver frame. The man wore a uniform and looked to be in his late twenties. Kirsten felt a wave of sadness. He would always, in Amy's mind, be in his late twenties. He had short hair that glinted blond and smiling green eyes and an open, frank face. What was it Jake had said? A Claymore mine …

She didn't enjoy the next few minutes, pulling open drawers, prodding and prying. When she was finished, she knew that Amy Montgomery was as neat and unrevealing in her personal possessions as she was in her public actions. Wasn't that, perhaps, peculiar in itself?

She opened Amy's door cautiously. Once again she surveyed the corridor, moved quickly across the hall and entered Drew's room.

The contrast was shocking. Drew's suite exuded an air of luxury from the deep pile of the carpet to the heavy, soft draperies and enormous, intricately-carved bedstead. Almost every inch of wall space was covered with paintings, mostly early Impressionist with their magical use of light. The chest and dressing table were cluttered with photographs, mostly of Drew: Drew fishing, Drew sailing, Drew climbing, Drew on the tennis court or golf course, the record of an active and vigorous life.

It was a wonderfully comfortable room with soft and deep armchairs. A welter of catalogs from stores all around the world from Harrod's to Neiman Marcus and announcements of sales and auctions lay in disorderly profusion on every table top. There was scarcely an inch of free space in Drew's room.

Kirsten looked about helplessly. This room could harbor a hundred secrets and she'd never find them. She searched cursorily, looking in his desk, a disorganized mess, and pushed a rack full of luxury suits to scan the closet.

When she left Drew's room, her initial impression of him was confirmed: Drew loved rich.

It was easy to walk downstairs and out across the terrace and meander casually toward the garages beyond the rose garden. A gardener worked near the pond but he was out of sight when she reached the steps that led up to the apartment above the garages that belonged to Murray.

Jake had given her a set of keys, but she didn't need to use them. Murray's door wasn't locked.

When she stepped inside the door, she stepped into another world. Every inch of wall space held campaign memorabilia, posters of Jake, campaign flyers, banners, even newspaper clippings. Kirsten wandered around the room and realized, at the end, that she had followed Jake's career from his very first race to the present.

There could be no question of Murray's devotion to Jake, but such total and unquestioning commitment might pose its own danger. Could someone have persuaded Murray that Jake needed special protection and that he, Murray, was part of a secret team to carry out dangerous assignments that would benefit Jake? She would have to talk to Jake. How much did Murray understand and how credulous was he? It could be critical to know.

Back in her room, Kirsten wrote a summary of her exploration, When she was finished, she shook her head in vexation. This wasn't accomplishing anything. They needed the resources of the CIA to fine-tooth comb the past of Amy and Drew and Murray. Nothing else would suffice. She frowned anxiously. Would Jake be able to convince Connor to look beyond her? How much time would they have before the Russians made a move?

16

JAKE STUDIED THE SPIRIT of St. Louis. It was so easy now to look back and wonder at the hoopla when a single man crossed the Atlantic for the first time in an airplane, but seeing that small, frail craft, scarcely more than wood and glue, brought home the bravery of that journey.

"I wouldn't ride in that to New Jersey," a voice at his elbow said.

Jake nodded in agreement, then he and Connor turned and walked casually to the left, unremarkable and unremarked in the swarm of tourists.

Meeting at the National Air and Space Museum had been Connor's idea. "Somebody might be keeping an eye on you," he'd said briefly.

Jake took a devious route to the hall and was certain no one followed.

While not seeming to, Jake surveyed Connor carefully. Damn the man's poker face. What was he thinking? More importantly, what was he doing?

Then, deciding he might as well force the issue, Jake demanded, "What's happening?"

Connor appeared deeply interested in a display of navigation equipment. "Not much, Senator. It looks like it will be mostly a waiting game for us."

Jake frowned. "Surely you're checking out what Kirsten told you. Haven't you discovered anything on the L.A. end?"

Connor peered at the scale model of an X-15 rocket-powered research airplane. "Not too much. We found the empty offices she says were used by the casting agency. Everything else she told us can't be confirmed." When Jake started to speak, Connor continued. "We spotted a woman of the right description who's a stenographer on the staff at the Russian Consulate. Funny thing is, we'd had a tip she might be involved in espionage."

"All right," Jake said warmly. "That's proof for Kirsten right there."

"Maybe." Connor's voice was totally uninflected. It was equally flat when he said, "We also found something the young lady didn't tell us about."

Jake waited and there was the beginning of a hard knot in his stomach. Why was Connor's voice so damn flat?

"Yeah," Connor continued. "We've been checking the girl out pretty carefully. So far everything she's told us is accurate, about her background, her family, her schooling. But she didn't tell us she'd deposited $50,000 in her bank account just before she left California for D.C."

Connor looked at Jake then and the CIA agent's gray eyes were speculative and observant.

Jake had grown up in a tough school of war and politics so his face didn't change, but inside he felt like he'd been kicked by a horse. At the same instant, he had a gut reaction: frame-up.

"It's like Kirsten said to begin with, she's set up to be the patsy."

"You think somebody deposited it in her account just to cinch the case against her?" There was just the slightest derisive note in Connor' voice.

"I sure do," Jake responded. "They wouldn't have any trouble getting a deposit slip or the number to her account. We already know they got into her apartment both in L.A. and Carmel to leave instructions."

"The girl didn't say anything about her things being searched."

"They're experts, for God's sake," Jake insisted, but he had the feeling he was pushing against a hard tide and not making any headway.

They walked on to the next exhibit and waited until a Cub Scout troop thundered past.

Jake faced Connor and frowned down at him. "I don't like your tone."

"I'm looking at this thing objectively, Senator."

The implication was clear.

"Listen, Connor, I'm looking objectively, too. Here are the critical points: only three people, four counting my mother, knew that I would be in California; only a member of my staff could have known I would be receiving the Amraam material by military messenger, and, finally, that personal information on me that they gave to Kirsten included a statement that I made only once in my life and that was in the presence of three people: my secretary, Amy Montgomery; my press aide, Drew Wilkerson; and my driver, Murray McCain.

Conners' face was impassive. "Senator, there are too many possibilities for leaks all around you. Who made the plane reservations? Who handled the assignment of the papers in the Pentagon? How talkative are the people who heard that particular remark?"

"You won't listen."

"We listen. We're looking at your staff." He pulled a packet of cigarettes from his pocket and lit one.

The clever goddam Russians, Jake thought. It was worth $50,000 to pinpoint suspicion. Still, the phony FBI agent wanted Kirsten to meet the contact and, so far as he knew, that would still be the *coup de grâce*. Jake had intended to raise hell with Connor about subjecting Kirsten to a meeting, but that meeting was the only hope of proving Kirsten was a victim, not a conspirator.

"Connor, I want you to go back to your office and study the transcript of Sunday's session with me and Kirsten. I want you to pay particular attention to her description of the black pickup that tried to force her off the road."

Connor stared at him and waited.

"Don't you see what that means?"

"You tell me, Senator."

"As soon as they thought she'd made contact with the Russian operative, they tried to kill Kirsten."

"So she says."

Jake ignored that. "The point is this: I want her covered like a blanket when they set up the contact."

"We'll cover her, Senator, don't you worry – if anybody sets up a contact."

He met Jake's gaze squarely. "We'll keep in touch." He turned and walked away.

Jake walked for more than an hour in the humid, enervating August heat. He liked to walk in Washington, in summer and winter. He loved the dramatic vista up Pennsylvania Avenue and he liked to walk across the rolling green lawns at the Washington Monument and stand and stare into the reflecting pool, but today nothing eased the cold realization that the CIA thought Kirsten was an active and willing KGB agent and her story fabricated to misdirect suspicion.

He felt a sharp pang of anxiety. What would happen if the Russians didn't call, if they didn't set up a meeting?

The limousine swept smartly over the 14th Street Bridge and past the Lincoln Memorial. Jake smiled and reached out to take her hand. Kirsten smiled in return. This should be a wonderful evening, to be alone with the man she loved, to feel the warmth and strength of his hand, to explore parts of this most glittering and cosmopolitan of cities. What happened here affected every citizen of every country in the world and this man who cared for her was a part of the power and the reality of this city.

It should have been a wonderful evening, but they couldn't escape the reality of their situation. Kirsten saw that in Jake's occasional quick frown. It was reinforced by their careful conversation. They talked about the weather and the upcoming Labor Day weekend. She knew he had information to report from his day in the Capitol and she, too, had her gleanings from her search, but they couldn't talk freely in front of Murray so there was constraint between them.

When the car eased to a stop, Jake said lightly, "This is a very famous watering hole, Kirsten, known as The Monocle. After the holiday is over, you can find somebody important here almost every night of the week. It's a favorite spot of Teddy Kennedy's."

The *maître d'hôtel* knew Jake, of course, and gave them a secluded table along a back wall.

She ordered a gin and tonic and he chose a scotch and water. They chatted lightly until the drinks came and then, when the waiter was gone, he leaned forward.

"Did you find anything?"

She shook her head, "I'm discouraged." She described her conclusions, said wearily, "But so what? I could have guessed all of that. The CIA's got to investigate. There has to be some trace somewhere, some link between one of them and the Russians."

Jake absently turned his drink around and around on the table. "They're looking. They're not finding much." He downed the rest of his drink and said firmly, "Look, we can't do any more than we've done, and, so far, the CIA is holding off against you so let's not worry about it, Kirsten, not tonight. Let's have tonight for us."

They talked of many things and they didn't talk of many other things. They looked into each other's eyes and there was much that would never need to be said.

They went to Georgetown for dinner and Jake's descriptions of some of his colleagues fascinated her, the Senator who collected Superman comic books but insisted they belonged to his son, the Senator who hated cats and was suspected of sharpshooting them by his Georgetown neighbors, and the Senator who included in every campaign platform hot rhetoric against pornography but who went often to an aide's apartment to watch X-rated movies.

"The moral is …" and she waited.

He grinned. "The moral is that life often isn't at all what it seems. I had a wonderful neighbor once when I lived in San Francisco, a very wry and canny old lady, and one of her favorite sayings was, 'They'll tell you anything.' A generic they. I remember that often. It's kept me out of a lot of trouble."

They finished dinner with a French pastry and Colombian coffee. Kirsten felt happy and safe and optimistic. On the ride back to Virginia, they sat close together, Jake's arm firmly around her shoulders. He kept his arm around her as they walked up the curving staircase, but outside her door he said, "If you're tired …"

She smiled and reached up and slipped her hands behind his head. "Never that tired, love."

His head bent and his mouth sought hers and there was as always and she knew it would always be so, a spark of excitement that crackled with the force of electricity.

Kirsten reached behind her and twisted the knob and her door swung in and she gently tugged at Jake.

When the door was shut again, he turned to her and reached for her hand. They walked across the floor to the bed and then they stood beside it and undressed each other and their clothes fell onto the floor and then they faced each other, their limbs a soft white in the gleam of moonlight through the unshaded windows.

Jake drew her close to him and they stood holding each other, treasuring the warmth and firmness of their bodies melded together. Their mouths joined and the prickly rush of desire flooded them and then their lips sought and their hands caressed and the ineluctable magic swept them. He lifted her then and she clung to him and welcomed him and felt a kinship with the hurtling passage of a comet, streaking magnificently through space.

"You are quite wonderful," he said softly when they stretched out on the bed.

"Only because of you," she replied.

As they fell asleep, his hand entwined with hers, Kirsten realized that she'd begun the evening anxious and afraid and now nothing seemed impossible. She and Jake would win out. She would never doubt it again.

Michael leaned forward. "It must be done."

The man behind the desk, Col. Dmitri Konstantin, was sallow-faced and thin and he moved his hands a very great deal when he was excited. He was excited now.

"My very dear Mikhail …"

"Call me Michael."

Konstantin's hands wavered in the air like pudgy butterflies. "This is not at all what you outlined to us originally."

"No one is more aware of that than I," Michael said bitterly.

"If anything went wrong, it could cause an incident, a very serious incident, and with the Chairman of the Supreme Soviet even now en route to a summit with the American President it could be a grave matter."

Michael had the authority to force his way, but it always paid to win cooperation so he forced a smile though he would have enjoyed pounding his fist into the thin, supercilious face of the military attaché.

"I appreciate your concern and, of course, it is important that we do nothing to lessen the Chairman's chances of success with the President. However, you know as well as I do that these political meetings come and go. The matter of most concern to Mother Russia is our defense and I do not need to tell you how critical it is that we receive these plans. They are almost in our grasp."

The colonel's thin face hardened. "Almost, my dear Michael? Why almost?"

The glaze of bonhomie slipped away from his round face for a revealing moment and anger flashed in his eyes. That damn young woman. Why had he ever agreed to the complicated scheme? But there had been no choice. His informant would provide the plans only if someone else to took the blame, and someone else was the blonde actress.

"We can't get the plans," he said shortly, "until we provide a dupe."

The colonel looked bland. "A dupe?"

Michael almost twitted him about his mastery of English, but, once again, his innate caution prevailed. Never make an unnecessary enemy.

"Someone to take the blame. We have to be sure that the woman is linked to us beyond question before we will receive the plans."

"Why not take the plans?"

Michael smiled but there was no warmth in it. "I certainly would do that, my dear Dmitri, if I could, but our informant is very clever and has made it quite clear we will never find them on our own initiative. Besides, if we protect our informant, there will be times in the future when we will be able to obtain most interesting information about the Senator and his intelligence activities."

That was one reason. Michael had no intention of telling Dmitri the other, the overriding reason. The informant knew Michael.

Dmitri lit a cigarette and blew a long plume of smoke that curled in the air. Then, frowning, he said importantly, enjoying his role, "Tell me again what you plan."

Jake glared at Connor. "What the hell do you mean?"

"Time's passing, Senator. Just like I said."

"Look, maybe the Russians never will make contact with her. Maybe something's scared them off."

"Like the lady?" Connor said softly.

Jake took a deep breath. It wouldn't help to explode at Connor. The man was just doing his job. The thing was, he didn't know Kirsten. That made all the difference.

"What are you trying to say, Connor?"

The CIA agent brushed his hand a little uneasily through his short, blond hair. "You and Miss Soderstrom … you kind of have an understanding, don't you?"

Jake was silent for a long moment, then he said quietly, "Yes," and thought it the most inadequate answer he'd ever made. But how could he explain to Connor? Would Connor understand a coming together that was so deep and complete that it defied explanation or description? Did Connor know about love, the kind of love that lifted your soul and gave you a glimpse of eternity? Did Connor know about passion and trust and sharing?

Then Jake realized Connor was talking and he'd missed part of it. He pulled his thoughts back to the present and listened and looked in dismay at the open box Connor held in his hand.

"You see, Senator, the trouble is she thinks everything's hunky dory. Now, if you'd indicate to her that we're getting ready to make a move, say by Monday or Tuesday, I think things might pop." Connor looked up at Jake, his eyes insistent. "And this little beauty could record the whole thing."

Jake felt a pounding anger inside, but he kept his voice even. "Wait a minute. You think Kirsten will …" he paused and swallowed, then continued, "… panic and try to run if she believes you're going to arrest her?"

"You bet." Connor's voice was dead confident. "If she gets scared, if she thinks the jig's up, she'll beat it and get in touch with her boss. Then we'll round them all up."

Connor held up the box. "This will record any conversation she has."

The box held a necklace on a thick gold chain. A locket hung from the necklace.

Connor touched the clasp and the locket opened. On one side was a picture of Jake and on the other, a silver medallion with an etching of Jake's yacht.

Kirsten felt uneasy on Tuesday when there was no word from the Russians, concerned on Wednesday, worried on Thursday, frightened on Friday, desperate by Saturday.

She stood on the bridge curving over the pond and gripped the railing. "Jake," and her voice was low and strained, "what if the Russians don't set up a meeting? What happens then?"

"I don't know," he said slowly.

She whirled around and reached out and clutched his arm. "What will the CIA do?"

He didn't answer and something in his silence frightened her more.

"Jake, tell me. You know something."

Slowly, he nodded. He hated to see the look of strain in her eyes. He hated not being able to be totally honest with her, but, as Connor had pointed out, a man sometimes had to do things for his country that weren't easy – and this was going to be one of them. He believed in Kirsten. He would always believe in her. It wouldn't matter if there were five million dollars in her bank account. He knew she was straight, and, more than that, he loved her and knew he always would. There would never be anyone else for him, never, but, when Connor insisted, Jake had agreed.

Jake knew Kirsten was innocent and this would prove her innocence, beyond all doubt.

"There's a tough problem," he said reluctantly.

She waited.

"There's $50,000 in your bank account in Huntington Beach."

She stared at him blankly then began to shake her head. "Oh no, that's silly. That's some kind of mistake. I had a balance of $27 before I put in the money that the agent, the fake one, gave me."

"How much money?"

"Two thousand dollars. I was supposed to get a thousand dollars a week."

"There's $50,000 in there now,"

She stared up at him and her eyes were suddenly pleading. "Jake, don't you see, they did it deliberately."

"I know. That's what I told Connor."

She scarcely breathed. "What did Connor say?"

"I'm afraid, if something doesn't happen pretty soon, I'm afraid they're going to arrest you Tuesday."

Well, he'd done it as Connor had demanded.

He hated the fear in her eyes and wished he could bring the words back. Dammit, why didn't the CIA find the people responsible for all this?

"I'd better go to a hotel," she said numbly.

He stared at her in surprise then felt an overwhelming rush of love, because he understood even before she explained.

"I'd better go right now. I can't be arrested at your house. That would be awful. That would be dreadful."

He pulled her into his arms then and held her tight. "Don't, Kirsten, don't. It's going to be all right. I know it will be. Don't be frightened. I think they're bluffing."

She began to struggle. "I'm going to leave this moment."

He held her tightly then, his hands clamped on her arms. "Hold up, don't panic. We'll take it one day at a time. Come on, Kirsten, we'll make it all right." He paused again and clenched his jaw and said gruffly, "I have something for you, something I'd like for you to wear."

He reached into his pocket and pulled out the necklace.

17

MICHAEL WIPED THE SWEAT from his face with a sodden handkerchief. How could anybody stand living in Washington? Even the short walk from his hotel to DuPont Circle left him gasping for breath and feeling as though he'd spent a week in a steam bath. When this was over, he'd get back to L.A. on the first flight. He ignored the uncomfortable constriction in his chest. It didn't do to worry. You started making mistakes when you worried. But deep inside he was very worried. When a deal started going sour, sometimes it went sour all the way. He was hanging out on this one. Still, if they got the girl, he would be covered – and they were going to get her. He glanced down at his watch and picked up his pace. He reached the sidewalk telephone kiosk just as the phone began to ring. He ducked inside, pulled the door shut and immediately began to sweat harder, with stinging moisture dripping into his eyes, slipping down his face and back and chest. Goddam climate.

He picked up the receiver. "Edelweiss Books?"

"Mercury here."

The identification phrases made, Michael said, "What's her schedule Sunday night?"

There was an instant's hesitation.

Michael barked, "Goddammit, talk. I'm sweating like a pig."

"There's a concert at the Washington Monument. The Beach Boys."

Michael forgot the stifling, humid heat in the telephone box and began to smile. "That's perfect, absolutely perfect."

"Wait a minute. I'm going to be there and …"

"Don't worry. Nothing bad's going to happen there." He wiped the sweat from his face and gulped for air, then said impatiently. "Now, look, when can I get the material? I'm getting some pressure."

"Not until the CIA's convinced beyond any doubt that she lifted the plans."

The connection was severed. Michael's face flushed dangerously. He shoved open the booth door. If he had any choice in the matter he would protect the girl and kill the informant. But he didn't have any choice.

He lumbered back down Massachusetts Avenue, wiping his face, ignoring the other pedestrians. A plan began to take shape in his mind.

It didn't take long to pack, because she had so few things. Kirsten folded the silk dress and tucked tissue around it and wondered why she bothered. It wouldn't wrinkle on the flight back to Los Angeles, but why should she care? She would never wear it again. It was the dress she'd worn the evening they'd gone to The Monocle for a drink, then to dinner in Georgetown.

She remembered the night so clearly, her distress and Jake's insistence that this one evening they would enjoy themselves, no matter what, and oh, they had. He had a sharp, incisive mind and she loved hearing his wry comments on the day's news. He was serious about his responsibilities, but he didn't take himself seriously. He was too aware of human frailty, too cognizant of the imponderables of human personality. He cared deeply about his country and her people, but he refused to believe that any one man or idea was indispensable.

Abruptly, Kirsten rubbed the back of her hand across her eyes. She mustn't cry. She knew what she had to do. She swept up her cosmetics from the dressing table and turned to walk back to the bed and her open cases.

A knock sounded on her door. She hesitated then called, "Come in."

Jake opened the door, then stopped short and stared at the packing.

Kirsten lifted her chin. "I'm going back to California."

"Why?"

She swallowed, then asked jerkily, "Did you see the morning paper?"

He made no answer, but he didn't need to.

The insidious words hung between them, palpable as the tension in the air. Kirsten would never forget the italicized paragraph in the gossip column: Is the Senate's most eligible bachelor about to take the plunge? But Washington worriers wonder – is the Senator sharing more than his bed with his new lady love?

Jake closed the door behind him and leaned back against it. His face was grave, his dark eyes drawn in a frown.

Kirsten wished she could walk across the room and take his face in her hands and kiss away the tension and the worry. He had never seemed more handsome, more desirable – yet more unattainable.

"It's just another ploy by the Russians, Kirsten."

"I know, but you have to face it, Jake. I can't stay here. Not any longer."

He pushed away from the door and crossed the floor in two strides and gripped her shoulders and she could feel his love and care in the firmness of his grasp.

"Don't go," he said urgently. "Give it a few more days."

She wanted terribly to stay. Even one minute more with him would be wonderful, but she was determined not to compromise his name. If, she thought bitterly, she hadn't already done that beyond repair.

Jake slipped his arms around her. "Look, we can't do anything about that stuff in the column. Tuesday, I'll get Connor to check it out, see if the source of the rumor can't be traced, but nothing can be done now, it's a holiday week-end."

She looked up at him and now she couldn't hide the tears in her eyes. "I can't bear it if I've hurt you."

"You haven't done anything," he said staunchly. "Nothing but show me once again what it means to love. It isn't your fault that we are caught up in something beyond both of us, but it will come right, Kirsten. The CIA's working on it right now." He hugged her hard. "So come on. Let's go to the concert and have a wonderful time and we won't worry about anything to-night."

American flags fluttered in the light breeze off the Potomac. The Washington Monument soared into the soft blue of the evening sky. Kirsten turned occasionally to look back at the Monument. She felt a swelling of pride as her eyes skimmed over the crowd. It was such an American crowd as Washington was such an American city despite the grandeur of its marbled halls and the breadth of its dramatic boulevards. She'd spent only a few days in Washington, yet she felt certain of its essence, a city of power yet a city open to inspection by the people it served. Tourists were everywhere, intent upon seeing where their representatives and senators worked, where their president lived. The concert tonight seemed perfect, a melding of superbly American music.

"Does it make you homesick?" she asked as the Beach Boys finished "California Girl".

"Absolutely," Jake responded.

Drew laughed. "How about a campaign shot on a surfboard? 'Course you might fall off."

Jake looked a little affronted. "I'll have you know, I know how to surf."

Amy said soothingly, "Drew's just teasing."

But Jake grinned, too.

Kirsten realized this was the most relaxed she'd ever seen the three of them. As the light faded, some of her happiness seeped away. She didn't listen to the distinctive, cheerful music with its evocation of sea and sun and sand. Instead, she felt a sweep of despair. Amy was keeping time to the music, her hand patting the soft fold of their blanket. Drew lifted a bottle of Heineken and took a deep drink and she could see the flush from the beer on his face in the fading light. Jake leaned forward, his eyes intent upon the bandshell, enjoying the moment, glancing at her occasionally to see if she were happy, too. How could she be happy?

The Russians hadn't contacted her, and she knew with a dull certainty that if they didn't she would never be able to prove any claims to the doubting Connor. What would happen then? She didn't want to face it, but the conclusion was inevitable. She couldn't be a part of Jake's life if she were implicated in the theft of important documents. She reached up and touched the locket hanging from the thick gold chain around her neck. Ultimately, would this be all she would have to remember Jake by?

Slowly, she looked down the gentle slope. It was filled with concertgoers, some stretched on the grass, others, like their party, comfortable on blankets with picnic baskets. It was a gay scene as the end-of-the-summer sun faded in the west, and Kirsten grieved for all the other happy scenes she would never be able to share with Jake. She longed to reach out and smooth down his thick hair.

He turned then and smiled at her and reached out to take her hand and she knew he'd felt her gaze upon him. She gave his hand a short, hard squeeze and determined not to think about tomorrow, to enjoy the moment as it existed and leave sorrow for tomorrow.

"Senator." The call was discreet, but firm.

Jake looked up at the Park Service ranger in surprise. "Yes?"

The young woman in the regulation olive drab blouse and darker green slacks bent down to say quietly, "You are requested to come to the Information Booth, sir, for a message." She nodded and smiled and turned to move away in the crowd.

For an instant, Jake's face was absolutely expressionless, then he smiled and said lightly, "Hope to God nothing drastic has happened in El Salvador." He jumped lightly to his feet. "Drew, if I'm detained, you'll see the ladies home."

"Sure."

Kirsten watched him move lightly up the slope until she lost sight of him in the milling crowds at the top of the hill.

It wasn't more than a minute or two when the uniformed ranger rushed up again to their blanket. She looked down and said with a trace of embarrassment, "I'm sorry, but you're supposed to come, too, Miss Soderstrom."

It was dark now, the only light spilling down the slope from the Monument and spreading out over the crowd from the bandstand, but Kirsten could see enough to recognize the surprise on Drew's face and the interest in Amy's. She didn't want to explain so she jumped up and said quickly, "Back in a minute," and turned to follow the ranger, ignoring Amy's call, "But Kirsten ..."

Kirsten was so intent on following the girl that she didn't realize their path was angling to the right. When they were deep in the crowd, out of sight by Amy and Drew, the girl turned, thrust a walkie-talkie at her and said, "Go down the hill toward the concession stand. Hold it to your ear."

Kirsten accepted the transmitter-receiver and obediently turned down the hill.

When the voice sounded over the set, she stumbled to a halt, then the familiar voice sounded again, so sharply and clearly, he might have stood at her elbow.

"Walk, Miss Soderstrom. Do not pause."

Kirsten looked frantically around and the voice sounded again, steely and cold, and she could picture him so clearly, sitting behind the desk of the casting agency in Los Angeles.

"You lied to me." She didn't know why she said it. It might have been the impulse to make it clear that she knew, that she wasn't a fool this time.

"We'll discuss that in a moment. I want you to walk down the hill and go just beyond the concession stand. A car is waiting for you."

Oh God, where was the CIA? Were they near? Was there someone watching this? They should have known the Russians wouldn't make an appointment with her, leave themselves vulnerable to a trap. Where was the CIA?

Still, Kirsten hesitated. Should she do as she was told, trust in the CIA to be watching? Then she remembered the black pickup truck and that dreadful moment when she'd known that her car was supposed to career off the cliff to smash into nothingness? She was afraid, yet she would do what she had to do if it would save Jake, but where was the CIA?

"You'd better hurry." The voice rasped from the transmitter. "Or the Senator has only twenty seconds to live."

For a dreadful moment, Kirsten thought she was going to faint. Her chest ached and she tried to draw breath into her lungs, strained to breathe.

"Nineteen seconds."

Kirsten turned downhill, began to walk fast and she held the transmitter to her face. "For God's sake, what do you mean?"

"Slow down, you fool, or someone will notice you."

Kirsten slowed and asked again, her voice shrill. "What do you mean?"

The sibilant, high voice whistled over the walkie-talkie and the words imprinted themselves on her brain. "Right now the Senator is walking toward the Information Booth and we have a high velocity rifle trained on him. At my signal, the marksman, and he is a very good marksman, will fire. The good senator's brains will explode."

"No." It was an animal sound, torn from deep within her.

"It's all very simple, young lady. You do as you are told, precisely as you are told, and I will not give the signal. Do you understand?"

"Yes. Please, I'm coming. I'll do it, anything, only please, don't shoot him, for God's sake, don't shoot."

"Shut up and walk."

The CIA agent wore khaki shorts and a tee-shirt. A bandana held back his thick curly brown hair. He scratched casually at his beard and ambled along about ten paces behind Kirsten. He looked young and slightly drunk and very cheerful. He wondered what she was doing with a walkie-talkie. But she was sure scooting along. You had to hand it to Connor. He had it figured, all right. Get the girl scared enough and she'd make a move. Be damned interesting to see who she met and what happened. He saw Connor in the crowd and Jim Kinney and their eyes slid past each other blankly. Looked like this was going to be an easy one. The lady was going to lead them right to the jackpot.

He was in the lead when they reached Constitution. Good. There was Prickett on his motorcycle and there were others laid on. He began to grin as he watched Kirsten step into a waiting Volvo that immediately accelerated. Well, they would be right behind that Volvo, discreetly, of course.

The driver didn't speak when Kirsten climbed in the back seat as she had been instructed. She sat on the slick, imitation leather seat and looked back at the Monument shining high on the hill. Jake was there somewhere.

"You won't shoot him?" she said hoarsely. "I came. I did ..."

"If you continue to do as you are told, the Senator will not be harmed."

Kirsten sat stiffly against the door. She didn't ask where they were going. It wouldn't matter. Wouldn't it help to tell them the CIA knew everything, knew about the casting agency and the meeting at Portsmouth Square and the angelic-faced boy on the California coast road? She huddled on the seat. No, not yet, not while they threatened Jake.

The car turned onto Fifteenth and swept alongside the east side of the White House and past Lafayette Park to turn onto H Street and then north onto

16th. Kirsten sat numbly. Her only feeling of surprise was the shortness of the drive and the sudden lurch of fear when the car turned abruptly into an alleyway, and the voice sounded again on the transmitter.

Jake stood in the center of the square office with a map of the District on one dun-colored wall. Connor faced him antagonistically.

"So what the hell would you have us do, Senator?"

Jake leaned forward on the balls of his feet. His dark face twisted with anger. "Why did you let them get her?" His voice was dangerously quiet.

Connor voice was low, too. "I didn't let them 'get' her, as you put it, Senator. She went with them, free as you please. She walked down to Constitution all by herself and got into a waiting car. It was planned, Senator."

"I don't believe it."

"Don't you? You should. You've been had, Senator. Frankly, I don't blame you. She's a gorgeous woman, but she's a wrong one."

"I don't believe it."

Connor shook his head in disbelief. "What does it take, Senator? A signed confession? As far as I'm concerned, she might as well have hand-delivered one. There can't be any question about it. She walked down and got into a car and drove into the Russian Embassy. You might as well face it, Senator, the show's over."

18

JAKE CROSSED THE FOURTEENTH Street Bridge, driving too fast, but he didn't care. It was almost midnight now and there were only occasional cars. Tomorrow would be Labor Day, a national holiday, everything closed, everyone at the beach or the ballpark. That was the American way and Kirsten ...

For the first time in his life, he felt helpless and terrified, more frightened than he'd ever been before. In Vietnam, there had been fear, the acid, curdling kind of fear that made you move tight-lipped and wary, but you moved, you knew what you had to do and you did it. But this – he faced an insurmountable problem and there was nothing he could do.

He turned left on 14th Street, drove to L and turned right and then left again on 16th Street. He drove slowly past the Russian Embassy. The front courtyard was dark. Scattered lights showed in the four-story building. Kirsten was somewhere in there and Connor had made his position very clear. So far as the CIA was concerned, she had gone of her own volition and her flight was proof of her complicity in an effort to gain access to classified material.

"She can't stay in there forever," Jake had retorted angrily.

Connor nodded. "True."

"Well, then, when she comes out, you can arrest her."

Connor looked at him strangely. "Is that what you want us to do?"

"I want her out of their hands."

"If she walks out, we'll be glad to. If she drives out, there's no chance. We aren't about to stop a car with diplomatic plates and try to arrest someone. It could turn out that she's sought asylum at the Embassy and all hell would break loose."

"I don't care what kind of stink ..."

Connor interrupted and, for once, he wasn't talking politely to a United States Senator. His voice was brusque and determined. "The Summit starts next Friday. We aren't going to do anything that could play into the Russians' hands."

Jake curved around Scott Circle and started back down 16th Street, and he suddenly felt such a wave of sadness and despair that tears burned his eyes. He knew in the depths of his heart that Kirsten was thinking of him at this instant, thinking of him and loving him, sacrificing herself for him. He didn't know how or why, but he knew that was her aim, beyond any doubt. Somehow, someway, he was going to save her. His head jutted forward in a pose his enemies and friends would recognize. The Mercedes picked up speed.

Kirsten lay on the narrow cot and watched the occasional flash of headlights as they swept through the narrow, basement room. The room had every convenience, a small bathroom, an easy chair, a comfortable one, even several books on a bedside table, but the books were in an unfamiliar language that Kirsten judged to be Russian and there was no exit from the bathroom except into the little room. There was a hall door but it fit securely and didn't budge when she tried to open it. She'd banged on the door for a while, but no one came and nothing happened and she decided the area was soundproof.

She knew the room was in a basement because there was a narrow window and when she looked out through thick glass and the iron bars beyond it she could see grass and, strangely to her, a set of exercise bars, and a curving drive and, past the shrubbery and several trees, still thick-leaved in August, a wrought-iron fence. Farther still, she glimpsed the street. She frowned in concentration. She was in downtown Washington, only a few blocks from the White House, being held prisoner in the basement of some building. How could her captors do this? What kind of building could be used in this way? Why were the books on the bedside table in Russian? But the questions and the answers didn't really matter. She knew who her captors were. The critical question, the question to which she had no answer and no inkling, was what were they going to do with her?

Kirsten clenched her hands and pushed up from the cot and paced back to the window. She held onto the low wooden sill. Maybe if she broke the window, but bars stretched to the top of the window.... She was trapped, well and truly trapped. She leaned forward and the glass pane was cool against her forehead, but nothing could ease the ache in her heart, the ache that was even worse than the fear. Where was Jake now? What did he think of her? She moved jerkily away from the window. As she did, the necklace he'd given her swung away from her neck. Kirsten reached up and touched the locket.

In a suite at the Capital Hilton, Jake sat grimly on the side of the bed, made one telephone call after another. He called Jesus Martinez in New Mexico, Harlan Mackey in Tennessee, Morey Kravitz and Frank Petrillo in New York, and Billy Joe Parker in Texas. It was shortly before one a.m. when he finished. Then he lay back on the bed, a pillow bunched behind him, but he was far from sleep. His eyes narrowed in concentration as he went over his plan in his mind. It could work, for God's sake, it could. Everything depended upon time. Could they all get to Washington before morning? He knew they were starting now, Jesus roaring down a narrow mountain road on his way to Albuquerque, Harlan en route to Nashville, Morey and Frank would be nearing Kennedy International. They would make it on time. Billy Joe would be driving to the Dallas/Ft. Worth airport. His men were coming. Now, all that remained was to get a room in the University Club, separated from the Russian Embassy by a narrow alleyway.

He kneaded his knuckles harshly against his temples. Had he forgotten anything?

Michael felt conspicuous as he walked up Massachusetts Avenue in the mid-morning sun. Two cars passed. One was a cab. It was a holiday morning. For a moment, anger wavered inside him again. If it weren't for that damned girl, he could be in L.A., down at the beach. He liked the beach, liked the anonymity of being part of the endless flow of humanity in Southern California. He didn't like being conspicuous. He reached the telephone booth and paused to tie his shoe, leaning down ponderously, aware that he was sweating again. All he did was sweat in this humid atmosphere.

The phone rang.

He snatched up the receiver. "Edelweiss Books."

"Mercury here."

Michael plunged to the heart of the matter. "All right, we've got her. Not it's your turn to cooperate."

"What are you going to do with her?"

"That's not your concern at this point. Look, I want to remind you," and his voice was as cold as the wind whipping the Murmansk harbor in January, "that we've paid you, paid you handsomely. It's time for you to produce, or she won't be the only one in a bad situation."

"It won't do you any good to threaten me. If anything happens to me – an accident or anything like that – I've left a letter with a friend that will be mailed right to the CIA, and you know something, it has a snapshot in it they might find very interesting."

Sweat beaded Michael's face and back and legs, but he felt suddenly cold. "A photograph?"

The voice was silky now and pleased with itself. "You remember how we met? At that bar in Carmel? I'm not such a fool. I knew you were cultivating me. I wasn't sure why, but I knew it wouldn't hurt to have a picture of you."

"I'll kill you."

"Not unless you'd like to see that picture on wanted posters all across the country." There was a pause. "Your bosses wouldn't like that."

Michael opened the door a little. He couldn't breathe. When he spoke, his voice was conciliatory. "Look, we've got to cooperate. Neither one of us wants to be found out. I'm doing my part. I've got the girl."

"What are you going to do with her?" The question was insistent, not to be denied.

Michael pulled the door shut again and the air in the booth throbbed with heat. He leaned closer to the receiver. "It's a perfect setup. She's going to go to Russia."

The silence on the other end stretched and lengthened, then the voice said sharply. "Are you playing with me?"

Michael swiped his sodden handkerchief over his face. "No way. Listen," and his voice dropped to a whisper, "it's all set up. Tonight the car will take her to the yacht basin and she'll be put aboard a waiting boat. It will rendezvous with a submarine tomorrow afternoon at three, well past the United States limit.

From there, the submarine will go directly to Murmansk. It will take a little over a week. When she arrives, they'll take her to Moscow and she'll be seen publicly with several high-ranking KGB officers. All of that information, of course, will go directly to the CIA. They'll be sure she's the guilty one. The thing is, we've got to transmit the plans now, too. If they don't show up in Moscow before she does, it's going to look very odd. It might set them to thinking."

Suddenly, there was low laughter. "The beauty queen's going to Moscow. I'll bet she won't like it."

Michael ignored this. "We must meet this afternoon."

"Not this afternoon. Tomorrow night, and I want a picture of her on board the submarine."

Each time the door opened, Kirsten felt a flood of fear. She was getting to know fear now, the way it constricted her breathing and made her heart thud erratically and caused her hands to perspire and her legs to waver. Fear was a familiar now, fear and a growing sense of hopelessness and, worse even than that, a feeling of non-being. No matter who entered the room, the middle-aged wiry man with her breakfast, the mustachioed man who came in mid-morning and did nothing but look carefully around the room, the tall, pale man who opened the door shortly after lunch to study her for a long moment— not one of them acknowledged her.

She spoke to each of them and hated her voice for being high. "Who are you? I want to leave here."

No one replied. No one met her gaze.

She was a non-person. She'd read that phrase before and, until now she'd had no sense of its horror, the devastating impact of being utterly ignored.

No one threatened her. No one hurt her, but her fear increased rather than decreased. When she was alone in the afternoon, she once again studied the room, searched out its corners, peered at the water-stained ceiling, but there was no chink in its armor. She was here and here to stay until her captors decided otherwise.

Each time the door opened, she steeled herself. She was going to struggle. She'd made that determination. She wasn't going to make it easy for them, but deep inside she wrestled with terror. She didn't know what they intended so she couldn't know when it would be best to make her stand.

The cellar room was air-conditioned. She spent the afternoon hours standing on tiptoe to look out the barred, ground-level window. Through the wrought iron fence and across the street, visible when the breeze shifted the oak branches, she saw a tattered sign hanging from the front of the opposite building, a dingy white banner with these words lettered in red: REMEMBER SOLIDARITY.

People disappeared without public outcry in Poland and in the Soviet Union. Could she disappear here in America? Was it going to happen to her? She was last seen …

Kirsten clenched her hands. Where was Jake? Didn't he care? But he would be like the rest of them, he'd think she'd run away.

Jesus Ramirez stood five foot four, stocky, his skin a rich, smooth bronze, his eyes a vivid, surprising green. He saw more than most men and he had an uncanny sense of danger. A tell-tale hoofmark would reveal a white-tail deer, a stealthy rustle among the firs a stalking bobcat. He could ride nervous horses and handle a drunk gringo with the same ease. Now he stood just to the side of the tall window in a room at the rear of the sixth floor of the University Club and looked through binoculars at the Embassy of the Union of Soviet Socialist Republics. Behind him on the bed, Harlan Mackey slept face down, his cowboy boots a startling reddish brown against the dull gold of the spread. Harlan rested so that when his turn came his eyes would be equally sharp and careful.

The binoculars began another slow and careful sweep. Nothing moved in the segment of alley that ran behind the Embassy, but that was where the cars were housed. One uniformed policeman stood on duty in the back alley. Another walked slowly up and down in front of the Embassy. Jesus would see him at the turn of his walk. Both policemen had motorcycles at hand.

The binoculars reached the end of the side alley that intersected 16th Street and ran between the Embassy and the University Club and swung back the other way. Abruptly, the binoculars held steady, then Jesus said sharply, "Harlan. Hey, Harlan."

They knew what kind of listening devices honed in on the Russian Embassy, monitored by both the Russians and the Americans, so the alert had to be short and, to those listening ears, meaningless.

Morey Kravitz lounged comfortably behind the wheel of the beat up Chevy, a good Jamaican cigar cocked between his teeth. He looked like a good-natured, enormous blond right tackle, probably a very slow right tackle, but when the message, "Derby Day," came over his walkie-talkie in Jesus's unmistakable New Mexican drawl, Morey had the motor on. The car moved down Fifteenth Street toward L. He noted The Washington Post on his right. Good paper, but it would sure be better for the lieutenant if this didn't make the next edition. Not the lieutenant now, the senator. Funny, it had never occurred to him when they were in Vietnam that someday Jake Johnson would be a senator and he would be back in New York, working his ass off to sell stocks. The thoughts trailed through his mind, inconsequential and fragmented, but his hands were rock steady on the wheel and his eyes were waiting for the car to come down L Street. He had to time it just right. The lieutenant had made that clear. They would have only a few seconds, no more than that. Then Morey saw the long, low, black limousine and he pressed down hard on the accelerator.

The Hertz rental truck started down the alley that ran behind the Embassy just as the limousine pulled out of the Embassy enclosure. Nobody gave the truck an extra glance, neither the uniformed policeman in the alley nor the occupants of the limousine. Murray drove the truck and kept a discreet distance behind the limousine.

In the truck van, Billy Joe Parker turned to Jake and he grinned, his huge, sunburned Texas face filled with delight. "Man oh man, here we go."

Jake nodded, but his face was grim and tightlipped. Would they hurt Kirsten? He didn't put the real fear into words. Life is so vulnerable. It can be destroyed in seconds, but they hadn't hurt her yet. Jesus's message meant that he'd glimpsed her in the car. She wasn't a body being transported, so if they could just move fast, so fast, move before the Russians could react. He balanced on his feet in the swaying van and hunched forward, every muscle taut.

Frank Petrillo, short, dark and bulky, put a hand on Jake's arm. "Hey listen, lieutenant, you stay in the van. You know Billy Joe and I can handle it. After all, you're a senator now. If it blew up, it wouldn't look so good for you."

Jake shook his head, once, emphatically. "I don't give damn. I'm in. We've got to move fast." There was a plea in his voice. "We've got to do it just right."

His words broke off because the truck, abruptly, jolted to a stop. It was time.

Kirsten sat stiffly in the back seat of the limousine— on her right the man she'd known as FBI agent Kemp, on her left the door, middle-aged man who'd brought her breakfast. She'd never seen the driver before. He had a thin, wrinkled neck and his uniform seemed too big for him. Again, no one spoke, no one answered her questions. It was when they were getting into the car that the heavy-set man from California warned her, "You will be quiet now." That was all he said, but she knew, without doubt, that she mustn't speak.

As the car pulled out into the narrow alley, she looked desperately around. Was that a policeman, there, to her left? But then he was gone, out of sight. It was too late, and she realized bitterly than an opportunity was lost. She must watch and be prepared. She must make some kind of move before the car left the District, though it was deserted. She remembered, as the car turned left onto L, a one-way, that this was Labor Day. There would be very few cars or people. That was probably why they were moving her now.

Suddenly, the driver shouted and slammed on his brakes and the limousine slewed to the left and the men on either side of her were thrown roughly against her, then all of them tumbled against the seatback. There was a grinding crash of metal. The car bucked and rocked.

Abruptly, the man from California slipped a fat arm around her neck and drew her head back. "Do not say anything, do you understand me, or …"

She dimly realized the driver was opening his door and a man was getting out of an old car and walking forward, saying in a harsh New York accent, "What the hell, mister, can't you tell when a light's red?"

The rest of it happened in seconds. The minute the chauffeur opened his door a truck pulled up beside them. The van door swung out, running figures reached the limousine. Two enormous men reached in and grabbed the men on either side of her and pulled them out onto the pavement. Then Jake was there. She knew him and she wanted to cry out his name and catch him and hold tightly to him, but he grabbed her hand, shouted, "Hurry, Kirsten, hurry." The sharp wail of a siren sounded in the distance.

19

JAKE PULLED KIRSTEN OUT of the car, pulled her with him to the Hertz truck. They jumped up into the van and slammed the door behind them. Murray gunned the motor. The truck lurched forward. They could hear the rising wail of a siren coming nearer and nearer. Jake held Kirsten tightly as the truck made a sharp turn.

"The men who were with you," she gasped. "We left them. Jake, we shouldn't have left them."

"It's all right. They had to hold onto the Russians, be sure they didn't pull out a weapon, but as soon as we drive off they'll beat it. There's another car for them parked around the corner."

"Won't the Russians shoot at them?"

He shook his head and said, lightly now, relief evident in his grin, "A bloodbath on L Street to celebrate Labor Day? No. What good would it do them? Once we got you safely away, they're done for. They can't say a word to the cops when they pull up. They can't exactly explain that they kidnapped a U.S. citizen, please, and these bad men took her away. We're home free, Kirsten." He looked down at her and the fear he'd battled through the long hours of the night and the day showed in his eyes and he pulled her into his arms and held her tightly and murmured her name over and over again.

Kirsten clung to him and tears began to slip down her face.

He felt their wetness and gently tucked his hand beneath her chin, "Don't cry, love. You're all right now."

"Last night …" and she spoke raggedly, the strain and horror clear in her voice, "they said they were going to shoot you if I didn't come."

He listened as she told him of the fat man's instructions over the walkie-talkie and his warnings.

"So that's how they did it," he said angrily. "By God, Connor will have to listen to that."

Then the truck slowed and stopped and Jake reached out to open the door.

Kirsten clutched his arm. "Should we get out?"

"Come on. They may be looking for the truck. Here," and he swung her down to the pavement and took her hand and in a second they were in the Mercedes and Murray was driving the truck off.

For the first time, Kirsten really began to believe they'd made their escape as Jake turned off Connecticut and curved around DuPont Circle onto New Hampshire.

She sank back against the soft, red leather seat.

Jake gave her a quick glance. "Did they hurt you?" he asked grimly.

Kirsten managed a smile. "No. They scared me to death. Oh Jake, it was awful. No one would look at me or speak to me." She shuddered.

Jake frowned. "They didn't interrogate you?"

"Nothing. Not a word. Nobody even acted like I was alive."

"Hell," he said shortly.

He saw her look of surprise. He hesitated, but it wouldn't do any good to tell Kirsten about the necklace. It would only disappoint her that she had nothing to help clear her, so he forced a smile.

"I'd hoped maybe you had some better idea of what they wanted."

Slowly, Kirsten shook her head. "I don't even know where I was." She twisted in her seat and said eagerly, "But you know, don't you? We can tell the CIA …" She stopped. "The CIA knew?

Jake knew his face revealed more than he wished. "Yeah."

"Why did you have to rescue me?" she asked sharply. "Why didn't the CIA arrest those people and free me?"

At least this was being picked up by the recorder, Jake thought. The puzzlement in her voice was so genuine, her confusion so evident. Yet, he could see Connor's sardonic reaction and hear the question, "She's an actress, isn't she, Senator?"

"The CIA couldn't do anything," he said quickly. "You were in the Russian Embassy, Kirsten."

She stared at him. "That's crazy," she said finally, "Really crazy. Why on earth?"

This question he didn't want to answer, but maybe the walkie-talkie instructions at the Memorial had been picked up by the recorder in the necklace.

"When the guy told you to keep on walking, was it loud on the walkie-talkie?"

Slowly, she shook her head. "No. I had to hold it right next to my ear to hear."

No good, he thought, *no good.*

They were across the Potomac now and the enormous complex of the Pentagon lay to their left. "Jake, why did they take me to the Embassy?"

He hated making the answer and he hated watching her face as he spoke. "To make it look like you were seeking asylum."

"Oh, my God." She stared at him, her face stricken. "Then the CIA thinks ..."

Slowly, he nodded.

She stared out at the night, at the blaze of lights on either side of the highway, then she said, very slowly, very clearly, "They'll arrest me, won't they?"

"No, by God. Look, Kirsten, I've got a plane ticket for you to Rio and a passport and ..."

"Jake ..." There was a kind of wonder mixed with despair. "You aren't thinking straight. You can't do that. Why, you could be charged with conspiracy and aiding the escape of a felon and obstruction of justice," and it was the prosecutor's daughter speaking.

"I don't care," he said determinedly.

"I care," she responded. "I care a lot. I'm not a traitor or a crook. I may have been a fool, but that's all. I'm not going to let them get away with it."

"Who?"

"Everybody. The CIA, that damn Russian, and whoever it is on your staff who set me up."

He slowed the car a little. "I know how you feel, but there's not a trace of proof that anybody did it. I know this much. It wasn't Murray, but I never thought it could be Murray."

It was Kirsten who spelled it out. "Drew or Amy, Jake. Amy or Drew."

"We don't have any proof, not a damn particle."

Kirsten shoved a hand through her hair. "All right, we don't have any proof. By God, Jake, let's get some proof."

It took time to fill out the accident report. It took time to assure the investigating police that no one was injured. Michael's face stretched in a smile that never reached his eyes. Cleverly done. Clever bastard, whoever planned it. The others, the huge, experienced, and very strong men who'd held the two of them and the driver immobile, had disappeared before the police arrived. All that was left was the blond man with the cigar leaning against the hood of the battered Chevy, insisting the Embassy car had run a red light. Very cleverly done, and it might spell the end of his career. A sharp pain burned briefly in his stomach. Would he be recalled or would they … He pushed the thought away because it never did any good to think about defeat. He had a superstition that thinking about defeat could bring it. And there was still a chance. The whole operation didn't look like a CIA maneuver so it had to be the senator, though it was hard to believe he'd risk his skin like that. If it was the senator, maybe he was going to take his girlfriend home with him. They could hope, anyway.

Finally, he was free and the limousine moved up the street. Michael directed the driver to Massachusetts Avenue and was dropped off and in a moment was in the confines of the telephone booth. He phoned directly. There wasn't time to do anything else. At least one piece of luck rode with him. The person he sought answered the phone.

Michael spoke quickly. "The person we were discussing recently who was scheduled to make a journey is perhaps en route there at the moment." He depressed the receiver. He stood in the hot booth, hot and smelly even in the Washington dark, and his cruel mouth spread in a genuine smile. He wished he could be there to see the finale. He didn't doubt one would occur. He took a deep breath. He wouldn't go back to the Embassy. He remembered the supercilious face of the military attaché. How he would enjoy this, but Michael didn't intend to provide that pleasure. He was a careful man. All he needed to do was reach Los Angeles. There he had a new identity that he'd created a long time ago – just in case. He had a good deal of money secreted, too, under that name in a Santa Monica bank. All he had to do was reach California.

The Mercedes was parked on the ridge opposite Jake's house. They could see the soft, mellow glow of lights spilling from the windows and it was perhaps even more beautiful at night than in the rosy wash of the sun.

"I don't like it," he said stubbornly.

"I'm not going to run away like a criminal," she said with equal stubbornness. "I'm going to walk up that drive and burst in the door and accuse both of them. Don't you see? It will work. The innocent one will be genuinely angry and the guilty one will be absolutely devastated when I come in."

Jake's hands gripped the steering wheel. "I wish to God Murray were here. What if I don't get back in time?"

"You will," she said positively. "I'll wait for half an hour. That will give you plenty of time to get into Falls Church and call Connor then get back."

"I don't like it."

"Jake," and she reached out and touched his arm, held it tight, "I'm not going to spend my life dodging around South America. I love you. I'm going to fight for you."

He reached out and swept her into his arms. They clung to each other for a long moment.

She felt his smile against her face. "You know something, Kirsten, you're a hell of a woman, one hell of a woman."

Kirsten rehearsed it in her mind as she walked up the curving drive, slipping from the depths of one shadow to another. The scene demanded dramatic intensity. She would succeed only if she startled Amy and Drew, broke through their conventional shells and forced an emotional response. Everything depended on her skill. She felt supremely confident. She was through running, through being on the defensive, and, surely, her appearance would be enough to terrify the one of them who thought she was safely hostage. She paused in the deep darkness beneath a fragrant magnolia and studied the front of the house. Light cascaded from the unshaded windows of the drawing room to her left. The curtains weren't drawn. Kirsten edged nearer and stood on tiptoe. The brocaded chairs were empty. Drew and Amy could be anywhere, of course, in the library, in the billiard room, in their own rooms, though it was just a little after nine o'clock.

Kirsten checked her watch again. She had another twenty minutes before she should make her entrance. She hesitated, then moved purposefully toward the side of the house. It would be even more shocking if she made her entrance down the stairs. She was watching her step, moving quietly, thinking about what she would do and how she would do it, but she never had a chance to give her performance.

The watching figure held a flashlight in one hand and the small, 22. caliber pistol in the other. When Kirsten began to skirt the house, her destination was obvious. The figure raised the pistol, and the trigger finger began to tighten; then, with an impatient head shake, the hand lowered. She was going to come in the side entrance. It would be better to wait, better to be certain she was alone. How had she come? In a car, obviously, but she must have left the car at the foot of the drive.

Was she alone?

That was the critically important question. It would be better to lie in wait at the side entrance and take her prisoner and then see what the situation was. Maybe she had come hunting for Jake. Thank God, he'd gone to New York. Obviously, he wanted to put as much distance between himself and the scandal as possible. That was a break.

The figure ran lightly down the central hall and turned toward the billiards room. A closet sat at the end of the hall near the side entrance. It took only a few seconds to open the door and slip inside, and leave the door ajar just enough to hear.

Kirsten hesitated at the side entrance. Should she wait a little longer? But there was no one astir in the house. She'd seen no signs of life through the windows with their undrawn curtains. It wouldn't hurt to go inside and be ready. Gingerly, she opened the door, an inch at a time. Then she slipped into the hall and walked lightly on the edge of the broadloom rug.

She was halfway down the hall when the voice ordered her to stop. Her heart thudded as she turned and faced that familiar figure. The face was different now, its usual pleasant expression lost in a twisted grimace that was so full of anger and hate that Kirsten fought away a sweep of faintness.

Slowly, Drew raised the gun, raised it until it pointed directly at her heart, and then he said, his voice corroded with fury, "You bloody bitch."

She stared at him and wondered that anyone could hide his true nature so successfully. Good old Drew, charming Drew. In her heart, she'd suspected Amy; jealousy and loneliness had driven her to hate the man who came back from Vietnam when her man hadn't. Instead, it was Drew.

"But why?" Kirsten cried. "Why? You're Jake's cousin. You have everything, money and ..."

"Oh no," he reported. "I don't have anything. Have you ever heard of poor relations?"

The venom in his voice made it all clear, years of jealousy, years of anonymity in the shadow of a cousin richer, handsomer, brighter, athletically more gifted, braver.

"The poor relation," he said bitterly, his voice corrosive. "I've fixed him now, haven't I, and made a fortune to boot. When they find you dead here, a suicide, and it leaks out that the plans were stolen, and I'll make certain it leaks out, he'll be ruined. I've got the last laugh. I'm the clever one. I planned it all. I set it up. I got you hired and I framed you. You bloody little bitch, if you'd just followed directions, but I've got the money for the plans and I'm delivering them tomorrow night, and you're going to play your last role."

She looked at him, at the wild, desperate gleam in his light blue eyes, at the clenched jaw, at the rock-steady hand holding the small but deadly gun. Death faced her. Death was seconds away.

Drew began to walk toward her now and she could read her death sentence in those pale blue eyes.

Kirsten knew she had only seconds left. She could read it in his eyes. He would grab her and hold her, and he was certainly big enough and strong enough to immobilize her, and then he would bring the barrel of the .22 pistol up to her temple and there would be an enormous pain and then nothing, no life, no love, no Jake, nothing at all. It would be easy to do, then he could put the gun in her flaccid hand and fire it again, into a pillow, and she would have the officialdom, a case of suicide, the poor girl was unbalanced obviously, and everything would be over.

Kirsten took a step back. "Amy," she cried. "She'll hear and ..."

"I told her Jake had called and wanted her to come into the office."

"The servants ..."

Drew smiled and it was a travesty of his old grin. "Jake gave them the holiday off. No one will be back until late tonight. God bless the massa."

Oh, how he hated Jake and he was coming closer now, inexorably closer, those light eyes mad with hatred but careful and canny and utterly determined.

It would do no good to cry that Jake was coming. There was no time left for her. He was set on his course and nothing would dissuade him. In a split instant, Kirsten made her decision.

She lifted her hands to her throat and wavered, then sagged to the floor.

Drew halted for an instant, then once again he smiled. She watched through slitted lids and controlled a shudder and lay limply on the floor and she could smell a trace of dust and floor polish and she wondered if those would be the last sensations of her life, but her mind was racing and she was gauging his approach.

When he stood over her, then began to bend down, the pistol coming lower and lower, Kirsten waited until his wrist with the gun was thigh-level then she unleashed an explosive kick. Oh thank God for all those arduous hours of cross-country running. The point of her shoe caught his wrist and she heard bone crack and a high squeal of pain and the gun flew through the air and cracked against the wall and a shot reverberated in the narrow hallway.

Kirsten was moving all in one fluid roll and she was up on her feet and scrambling down the hall. She grabbed up the gun, then whirled to face Drew. She held the gun out straight. "All right, Drew. This is the end of the line."

He leaned against the wall, cradling his arm, breathing heavily. His eyes were still wild and glazed with pain and the beginnings of fear. He grunted unintelligibly, then turned and began to run heavily toward the door.

Kirsten raised the pistol, aimed it at his back and cried, "Stop. Stop or I'll shoot."

20

JAKE FOUND HER HUDDLED in the hall, her face streaked with tears. The gun dangling from her hands.

He pulled her up and said frantically, "Are you all right? For God's sake, Kirsten, what happened?"

"I couldn't shoot. I couldn't do it." She looked past Jake at Connor, his face impassive. "It was Drew," and she almost shouted it. "But he'll get away with it, won't he? You won't believe me and he can walk back in here tomorrow and say I'm lying and that will be it, won't it?""

Jake gripped her shoulders. "Kirsten, wait a minute. Did you confront Drew? Is that what happened?"

"He captured me." She spoke dully now, tiredly. "He admitted it, all of it, how he set up the fake sting and took the plans …"

Jake gave a whoop. "He admitted it? He told you?"

Kirsten gave a bitter shrug. "So who will believe me? Nobody ever …"

Jake grabbed her up and swung her around the narrow hall then hugged her hard and put her down and reached out and lifted up the necklace that hung around her neck.

"Kirsten, baby, it's all in here, every syllable of it." He slipped the necklace over her head and turned to face Connor. "Take it – and get busy."

Kirsten stood in the hallway and looked up at Jake and suddenly she understood, understood and her heart plummeted.

Once again, she'd been set up, this time wired for sound. All of Jake's concern was manufactured. Obviously, he thought she was guilty and he'd given her a necklace not because he cared for her but because he hoped to help entrap her for the CIA. He'd reported her arrest was imminent then given her the necklace. Yes, that showed what he thought, didn't it? She looked up at him, her eyes blazing. "That necklace was meant to trap me, wasn't it? No wonder you wanted to know what was said to me at the Embassy. It must have been really disappointing that I didn't incriminate myself. Now it turns out I didn't have anything to do with it, but I see what you believed."

She turned then and, rather unsteadily, moved down the hall, away from him.

"Kirsten. Kirsten!"

She didn't stop even though her heart was breaking.

The apartment at Huntington Beach was dusty and strange. Kirsten stood in the middle of the little living room. Was this going to be her life?

It was all the life she had. She had to pick up the pieces, start over again. She was right back where she started, broke and out of a job. The CIA had impounded the money she'd been given, of course. This afternoon she would get a copy of *The Hollywood Reporter* and start making the rounds.

She was a good actress.

Did she even care anymore?

She couldn't stay in the little room. Images of Jake moved in her mind, Jake standing on the deck of his cruiser, Jake smiling at her so gently and lovingly in the soft light of early morning, Jake running toward the Russian limousine.

Kirsten changed into her swimsuit and pulled on a robe and grabbed up her beach chair. On the beach, she dropped the chair then turned to stare out at the glittering blue water, knowing that it was a highway of adventure from Huntington Beach to Singapore and not caring at all.

"Kirsten."

She stood quite still, not turning. She didn't need to turn. She would know that voice anywhere, that deep, compelling voice. She would know his voice in the far reaches of heaven or the depths of hell, but it was shaken now with emotion. Then he was beside her and his hands touched her shoulders and turned her until they faced.

She couldn't see him very clearly because the sun was blazing behind him, but she knew him. Oh yes, she knew him, knew the way he walked, knew the long wonderful length of him.

"They caught Drew," he began without preamble, "and the man who hired him, some guy who ran a used car lot in L.A."

She didn't reply. She wanted to tell him to leave, she wanted to tell him that love couldn't live without trust, but she didn't have the strength. He was too near and she cared too much.

"Kirsten," and his voice was so soft, as much of a caress as ever a touch could be, "I never thought you were guilty. Never. I gave you the necklace because I had to, but I was sure that it would only prove what you'd been saying."

The words punched through the wall she'd built around her heart and she realized with a feeling of shame that Jake had done just as she had when she'd continued to work, as she thought then, for the FBI. She hadn't thought him guilty. He hadn't thought her guilty.

"That's why I searched your safe," she said haltingly.

He began to smile. "Can we go back to square one?"

She still wasn't sure. "You don't like actresses …"

"Right," he said agreeable. "I don't like actresses. But I like the hell out of one actress, one particular, brave, fine, wonderful actress."

Then she was in his arms, laughing and crying all at once. She knew there would be time now for all the words that hadn't been said, but none of that mattered now.

"Jake, oh Jake …"

His mouth closed over hers and they held each other tightly and the road to adventure ended where it began, in the sand on Huntington Beach.

About the Author

Carolyn Hart's books have won Agatha, Anthony, and Macavity awards. She has been honored at Malice Domestic as Guest of Honor and as winner of the Lifetime Achievement Award. She has twice appeared at the National Book Festival in Washington, D.C. *Letter From Home*, a stand-alone WWII novel set in Oklahoma, was nominated for the Pulitzer Prize by the Oklahoma Center for Poets and Writers. In 2014, she was named a Grand Master by the Mystery Writers of America. She lives in Oklahoma City with her husband, Phil.

You can learn more about Carolyn and her books by visiting her website: www.CarolynHart.com